"Want to help decorate a tree?"

"I'd like that," Adam said quietly, his eyes following Holly's quick, precise movements as she flitted from one side of the tree to the other.

"We're almost ready for the bears," she announced.

"Fine." He moved closer to the tree. "You know," he said pensively, "you're the first person I've met in Dallas, outside of the office."

"Business must be good." Holly's voice was muffled as she bent over the mound of bears. "Here, take these for me and start hanging them on the back of the tree by the window."

Something flashed in Adam's eyes as he took the armful of bears.

"Please," Holly added belatedly. "You have to watch me or I'll start treating you like one of my sisters."

Adam raised a black brow. "Not for long, you won't."

Heather Allison, who lives with her husband and two young sons in Houston, Texas, used to write letters, which she describes as "hysterical sagas," to family and friends when she was in college—letters they enjoyed enough to share with complete strangers! She began to hear, "You ought to write a book." So eventually, she did . . . She got the idea for *Deck the Halls* one hectic Christmas season, when she had too many musical performances (she plays piano and viola), her Christmas cards weren't sent, her shopping wasn't done, it was ten o'clock at night and she had three dozen cookies to bake for the next day—and a three-month-old baby with colic. Christmases since have been a lot more peaceful!

DECK
THE HALLS
Heather Allison

Harlequin Books

TORONTO • NEW YORK • LONDON
AMSTERDAM • PARIS • SYDNEY • HAMBURG
STOCKHOLM • ATHENS • TOKYO • MILAN

ISBN 0-373-03091-6

Harlequin Romance first edition December 1990

To my parents,
Boyd and Colleen Wilkes,
who taught me I could do anything,
then insisted I try.

Okay, Mom,
now you can say,
"My daughter, the author."

Printed in U.S.A.

CHAPTER ONE

"I NEED A HUNDRED and fifty polar bears." Holly Hall paced as far as the phone cord would let her. "I need them right now!" She stopped abruptly then took a deep calming breath.

"Yes, I know you close at eight, but this is an emergency and right on your way and—" She listened, eyes shut tightly in annoyance. "All right . . . yes, I understand."

One eye opened to glare at the partially decorated Christmas tree. She plucked off an innocent brown teddy-bear ornament and glared at it, too. "If a hundred bears are all you've got, fine. I'm in the Meecham building—the penthouse—and please, please hurry."

Holly had begun to hang up the phone when a loud chattering made her jerk it back to her ear. "What? But Mrs. Bloom—" She stopped abruptly, not daring to antagonize her best supplier. Besides, she'd already exhausted all the others.

"Yes, I'll pay you now. Well, by check . . ."

"And have it bounce all the way to the bank?" Mrs. Bloom's grating voice screeched in Holly's ear.

"We're doing better this season, Mrs. Bloom." Holly ignored the familiar flush of humiliation that stung her cheeks. She gripped the receiver. "Deck the Halls hasn't bounced a check all year. And you know I always pay you back as soon as I get the money." Holly kept her voice coolly professional and took out her frustration by yanking off the bear ornaments.

"That you did," Mrs. Bloom wheezed. "But who's to say this check will be good? Your credit's shot. I gotta eat, ya know."

You haven't missed a meal in thirty years, Holly wanted to say. She also wanted to slam down the receiver and never deal with this cantankerous old woman again. And she would have, if she didn't need those darn polar bears.

"The bank's closed and I don't have that much money in my purse. I've got to have those bears tonight." She hated begging.

"Do you now?" Mrs. Bloom fell silent, making Holly wait. "Cash, or nothing."

Holly stared at the gorgeous but nearly naked white-flocked Christmas tree. "I'm doing the decorations for *Town Square*'s Christmas issue. People might want to know where I buy my ornaments." Holly swallowed and licked her dry lips, hoping her unspoken implication would be enough to sway Mrs. Bloom.

Silence.

"So, if you could bring those bears to me and some of the little black top hats—" she gulped in a quick breath "—I'd...I'd be willing to pay extra," she finished in a rush.

Mrs. Bloom cackled. "You must be in a spot, sure enough. Last-minute job?"

Holly raked her fingers through her curly brown hair and sent an agonized look heavenward. "No," she mumbled, wishing Mrs. Bloom wouldn't enjoy the torture so much. "Whoever is staying here," she explained glancing toward the nearest bedroom, "will be back at ten o'clock. The photographers are coming tomorrow morning."

"Get one of your sisters to pick 'em up."

Another deep breath. The smell of new fabric dye and fresh paint was beginning to give her a headache. "They're on another job right now."

Holly snatched the last bear off, threw it on a white silk sofa and kicked one of the boxes filled with tiny, medium and large brown bears. What idiot had chosen that theme for this elegant apartment?

A professionally decorated Art Deco penthouse, with a breathtaking view of the Dallas skyline, shouldn't have cutesy brown bears cavorting on the Christmas tree. This was a place of shiny black and white, punched with red and silver—and she had an absolutely *perfect* Art Deco tree in her portfolio.

Well, the scheduling sheet did say the law firm had chosen the bears, but at least she could change their color—if only Mrs. Bloom would cooperate. Detestable woman. At least she hadn't prattled on about how the "mighty had fallen" again this year.

"I said, maybe we could work something out." The voice boomed in Holly's ear.

Holly shook her head slightly, suspecting what would come next. Smiling wryly, she decided to get it over with. "Got a fancy party coming up?"

"Ruthie's wedding. Herman's niece? She's marrying the Battley boy. You know him?"

"No," Holly said faintly.

"Course you don't," Mrs. Bloom continued, undeterred. "I wanna look nice. Herman's people always look down their noses at me. So I wanna look nice. You know what I mean?"

Holly squinted at the bears and thought about the photo spread in *Town Square* magazine. Her biggest break. Free advertising... "You want to borrow Mama's necklace again."

Mrs. Bloom's smile was nearly audible. "Call it collateral until your check clears."

Holly thought briefly of the diamonds sparkling around her mother's neck and sighed softly. "Let me give you directions to the penthouse."

She allowed herself the luxury of slamming down the receiver—after giving detailed directions to both Mrs. Bloom and her husband, Herman.

"Old bi—" Holly stared at the phone. "No," she said thoughtfully. "Battle-ax." She tried the word again. "Battle-ax." *That* was Mrs. Bloom.

Now for the tree. Holly collapsed on the sofa, grabbed the teddy bear and absently tossed it from hand to hand. "You and your friends will have to go," she said to the ill-treated bear as she surveyed the boxes of decorations she'd brought.

The green plaid ribbon was also out for this room; there weren't even any plants. She got up and scanned the living area, trying to see it through the photographer's eyes. The tree would stay in front of the massive windows to capitalize on the fabulous view, no doubt about that. It was too bad the magazine people were coming in the morning; with the colors in this apartment, a night shoot would have been spectacular.

Holly glanced at her watch, then dragged both hands through her hair. Two hours wasn't enough time to do the kind of job she wanted. This Christmas tree had to be perfect. No, more than perfect.

Not that she was complaining. This was a good year, but it could be better—it *had* to be better. And she didn't need a couple of hundred cute bears giving her trouble, either.

Now, what could she salvage? Holly studied the tree. She'd keep the tiny white fairy lights. Thank heavens the tree was heavily flocked with white. Unfortunately the green plaid tree skirt was the only one she'd brought. It would have to go, and so would the gold beading. She ripped the strands from the tree, thinking furiously. Dumping the handful of beads into a box, she looked through the extra odds and ends she'd brought with her.

"Yes!" She pounced on the new silver ribbon she'd ordered. She'd use it to make the big bows that were a trademark of her Deck the Halls Christmas-decorating firm.

As her fingers flew over the ribbon and wire, Holly smiled to herself. Bows weren't that hard to make, but they didn't store very well. On the other hand, they were lightweight, which counted for a lot, and filled the gaps in nature's less-than-perfect trees. Deck the Halls couldn't afford to own more than a few artificial trees. In her typical fashion, Holly had turned this into an asset and boldly charged more for decorating "real" trees.

The buzzing of the intercom broke the silence. Holly collected her checkbook and the key to the private elevator on her way to answer the intercom. "I'll be right down," she told the security guard.

A couple of disgruntled Blooms stood beside the guard's desk.

"You and your sisters up to your fancy ways again, young woman?" Mrs. Bloom's nose was in the air.

"Everyone entering the building has to check in with the guard, Mrs. Bloom." Holly smiled sweetly. "As an employee, I just follow orders."

The thought of Holly as an employee apparently mollified Mrs. Bloom.

Holly gestured toward the two large clear plastic bags. "I hope the bears aren't all crushed," she said, then wished she hadn't spoken.

"And beggars can't be choosers, can they?"

"I'd hardly call it begging, at your prices," Holly muttered as she reached for the sacks.

"The necklace?" Mrs. Bloom snatched them back.

"I don't have it here!" Holly's patience was nearly gone. "Mama's necklace is at home. Come by tomorrow morning."

Mrs. Bloom eyed her shrewdly. "Thought maybe you'da run home and got it by now."

"Then I would've been able to get the bears, wouldn't I? Besides—" Holly looked her right in the eye "—it makes me nervous to carry it around at night by myself."

Mrs. Bloom snorted. "Hmph. Your mama wore it at night. I still got that picture that was in the paper, the one of her and the governor dancing at the inaugural. Gonna take it to Ruthie's wedding."

Herman Bloom winked at Holly. "Nobody'd believe them sparklers was real otherwise," he said in an undertone.

And they'd be right. Holly kept a smile plastered on her face as she lugged the two plastic sacks of bears into the penthouse elevator. "Mama's diamonds have more of a social life than I do," Holly complained to the bears as the elevator whisked them up to the penthouse.

Holly pushed up her sleeves and dragged the bears to the Christmas tree, then dumped them onto the floor. Hands on her hips, she surveyed the immaculately decorated room and the mess she left in front of the windows. She had managed to get the bears, hadn't she? Holly glared at them defiantly as the image of Mama's diamonds twinkling among Mrs. Bloom's chins came to mind.

Mama, of all people, would have understood. Laughing suddenly, Holly scooped up a handful of the bears and tossed them over her head.

IT HAD BEEN A LONG DAY. Adam Markland loosened his tie and leaned against the plush walls of the elevator. He closed his eyes and stood for a moment after he heard the doors swish open.

When he finally opened his eyes, he saw an angel—no, an elf—sitting in the middle of his living room. The sound of her laughter filled the quiet as fuzzy balls rained down on her curly brown head.

He smiled, revealing deep dimples. What was she doing here, this elf? This nicely shaped elf, he noted, watching her jump gracefully to her feet to gather the balls.

Holly turned off the lights, leaving the room in darkness except for tiny white lights twinkling on the Christmas tree. Nodding to herself, she flipped the room lights back on and turned in his direction.

"Oh!" She stopped and looked at her watch, then back at the dark-haired man lounging against the elevator door.

"I've been trying to think of something witty to say. With all of this—" he gestured as he advanced into the room "—there's bound to be a great line somewhere, but I'm so tired, I'm afraid you'll have to settle for 'Hi, I'm Adam Markland.'"

"Holly Hall, with Deck the Halls." Holly automatically extended her hand and looked straight into impossibly blue eyes. His dazzling smile, bracketed by deep dimples, made it unthinkable not to smile back. Her internal quality-control alarm went off.

Holly had a Texan's firm handshake. She noted the approval in Adam's eyes as he held her hand longer than good manners required. "What are you doing with the bears?" he asked, still smiling. She gently tugged her hand away, and laughed, then stuck both hands in the back pockets of her jeans. "I'm decorating for the photo shoot tomorrow." She quirked an eyebrow at him. "I don't suppose you were the one responsible for choosing these bears?"

Adam glanced down at the fuzzy brown sea at his feet. "No," he replied shaking his head, "I didn't choose the bears. Not that I have anything against bears," he added, covering all possibilities.

Holly frowned. "Neither do I, but brown bears don't go here and we had the perfect— Well, never mind. Anyway, I'm changing them to white—that's why I'm running late. I thought I had until ten o'clock." There was just a hint of accusation in her voice.

Adam gestured expansively. "As the sole occupant of the penthouse suite, I grant you permission to stay. How about some help? I'll be with you in a minute." He walked quickly to the nearest bedroom, ripping off his tie on the way, not giving her a chance to refuse.

Holly sank back into her pile of bears and stared at her fingers. Those couldn't be tingles. And if they were, it was because he'd gripped her hand too hard.

Mindlessly she grabbed a brown bear, pulled off the perky red bow around its neck and retied it to one of the polar bears. In spite of herself, she kept glancing toward the door through which Adam had disappeared.

The bow was crooked. Sighing faintly, Holly threw back her head and stretched her arms, then hooked her hands behind her neck. It had been a long day. Not for the first time, she wondered how Laurel and Ivy were doing with their tree. They'd insisted they could handle the decorating job alone. Holly smiled wryly. Her little sisters were growing up.

Adam paused in the doorway, tugging on a pullover sweater. "I've been doing that for the past hour, myself," he said, kneading the back of his neck before raising one hand and carelessly pushing back a lock of black hair.

Holly opened her eyes at Adam's approach and got another mental jolt. *Not now.* Not in the middle of the Christmas season. Besides, she thought she'd turned off quality control long ago.

"Are we tying bows here?" Adam squatted with difficulty. "Not broken in yet," he offered by way of explanation, grimacing at his jeans.

"Unlike these." Smiling, Holly gestured toward her own.

"Yeah." Soft from repeated washing, they hugged her lovingly. Holly studied him as his eyes unabashedly traced her curves, then flicked back to her face.

The pale blue of his sweater was a perfect foil for his cobalt-black hair and sapphire-blue eyes. Did he know that? Holly took inventory of his dark brows, his dimples and the tiny cleft in his chin. She liked the way his growing beard shadowed his face, giving it a rough look that contrasted with the soft sweater. Cashmere. Holly knew cashmere.

Adam picked up one of Holly's bears and she immediately realized she'd been staring. Feeling chagrined and a little embarrassed, she burst into speech.

"You don't have to help me if you don't want to. The law firm hired me to do this. It's my job." Now, why did she say that? She was desperate for him to stay. No, she wasn't. She didn't have the time or emotional energy to get involved with anyone.

"I want to," Adam said deliberately, his eyes holding hers.

All thoughts of insisting on her independence and self-sufficiency fled from Holly's mind.

They sat cross-legged, tying bear bows and exchanging unimportant tidbits of information about themselves. Holly decided there were enough red bows and began tying black and silver ones. She wanted to avoid looking at him. He sat there, surrounded by fuzzy bears, his long slim fingers tying elegant little bows around tiny furry necks. He seemed remarkably at ease.

"The brown bears and anything with green on it goes back in the boxes. How did you luck out and get to live in a place like this?" That seemed another in a series of safely innocuous questions. Holly knew that suites like this were often used for out-of-town clients, and she figured Adam would launch into a discussion of whatever company he worked for and its dealings with the law firm.

"The living arrangements are only temporary. Or they're supposed to be." He laughed lightly. "I'm the new partner at Swinehart, Cathardy and Steele. I came down from Boston a couple of months ago and haven't had time to find a place of my own yet." Adam was about to add more when Holly's rigid posture and frozen face stopped him.

Her eyes, a deep brown, were opened wide, and she didn't bother to hide the dislike flooding them. "So you're one of the stealing swine?" Each word was an icicle.

Adam didn't laugh. "An odd way to refer to the name of the firm that hired you."

"A rather appropriate name, I've always thought."

"You've dealt with us before." It was more of a statement than a question.

He was treading very carefully. Just like a lawyer, Holly thought scornfully. She went back to strangling bears and didn't speak immediately, feeling a sharp disappointment. She'd been betrayed by blue eyes and a pair of dimples. "This is the first time...professionally." There was bitterness in her voice and she knew Adam could hear it.

She'd nearly choked when the law firm hired Deck the Halls, but she was a professional, and successful professionals didn't let emotions interfere with sound business decisions. Wasn't that what Mr. Steele told her when he'd refused to represent her case several lean Christmases ago?

Holly finished the last bear, tossed it at the others and watched as it bounced and tumbled down the mound. "A partner, no less," she said, looking at him directly.

"Yes." Adam nodded, his eyes assessing.

Holly hated it when lawyers did that, closed off their faces and gave nothing away, all the while conveying the impression they were privy to the secrets of the world. "I thought you might be a client. Or maybe a specialist here to testify."

"I'm not a trial lawyer," Adam offered, trying to ease the tension. "I'm a bankruptcy lawyer."

Holly's face whitened briefly and she turned away, gazing out at the skyline. "Lots of bankruptcy cases in Texas now."

Adam sat with his arms looped around his knees. "Not as many as there were."

Holly's eyes swiveled back to him. She owed him an explanation. It was just such a shock to learn he was one of *them*. "I haven't had very good experiences with lawyers."

Adam studied her. "Nasty divorce?" he asked in an impersonal tone. "Or was your husband the lawyer?"

"I've never been married." She said it without apology, but her staccato tones warned him not to pry.

Adam felt inwardly cheered at finding out that she was single. So, she hated lawyers. From the tight look of her lips, it was going to take an abundance of charm to melt away the icicles.

With that thought in mind, he strolled over to the fireplace and lit the log he found there. It was one of those fake ones, the kind that didn't burn very long. He stayed by the fireplace longer than necessary, since the log caught fire so efficiently, and considered how to approach Holly. He wanted to get to know her. She had a direct quality that attracted him and her brown eyes had assessed him without coyness. He liked women who didn't play games.

She was the first woman he'd met who wasn't a fellow lawyer since he'd come to Dallas. He knew Holly hadn't been indifferent to him. Adam sighed, not caring whether or not she heard him, and poked at the log, which didn't need it. As he slowly replaced the poker, his fingers traced the elegant engraving on the pewter fireplace tool rack: S.C.S.—the Swinehart, Cathardy and Steele logo with its flowing script. The log shifted and the fire popped. It was a loud silence.

Stop being such an ass, Holly. Now that she'd created the uncomfortable silence, it was up to her to break it. She knew all lawyers weren't like the rich, parasitic vultures who had fought over the remains of her father's estate for the past four and a half years. And so far, Adam hadn't exhibited that cocky I've-got-you-right-where-I-want-you attitude, either. He'd even been helping her—without charge. That alone put him in a different category.

Gathering an armful of silver bows and garlands, she approached him. "My parents always put colored sprinkles on our fires." She gave him a tentative smile and was rewarded with a breathtaking one in response.

"So did mine," he said his voice rich, velvety.

"A fire in the fireplace made it a special day." With difficulty, Holly dragged her eyes away from his and watched the dancing flames. Why was it so difficult to think all of a sudden?

Adam laughed. "Yes, it does take the chill off the air-conditioning."

Holly joined him in his laughter, her brown eyes reflecting the warmth of the fire, her brown curls glinting with copper lights from its flames.

"That's better. You have a nice laugh." Adam closed his eyes and inhaled. "You even smell like Christmas."

Holly grinned at him, revealing faint dimples of her own. "It's frankincense. It helps me get in the holiday mood." She indicated her armful of silver. "Want to help decorate a tree?"

"I'd like that," Adam said quietly. "I'll miss out on all that in Boston. Won't get home in time."

They stood in front of the tree and Holly handed Adam a bow triple the size of the rest. "This one goes on the very top."

Adam climbed the stepladder, leaning over as far as he could. "Is it straight? I can't tell from here."

"Yes, but be careful," Holly warned. "The tree is so full, I've been wondering how I was going to get the bow up there."

Adam finished securing the bow and gingerly straightened. "I assumed you'd have a giant bear sitting on the top."

Holly busily fed him more bows. "A Deck the Halls tree is always topped with a bow. We do make exceptions for angels, but then we have tiny bows surrounding them and ribbons hanging from those. But every other theme has a bow. I had a great one for the brown bears. It's just a simple bow with bears sliding down the streamers. Move that one over a bit."

"How's this?"

"Great!"

Adam looked down into her pleased face and caught his breath.

Holly was chatting merrily away, apparently putting her earlier animosity aside. "This is really going to work. I had my doubts and we don't usually go overboard on the bows, but I just couldn't leave brown bears on the tree, could I?" Holly looked to Adam for confirmation and flashed a quick smile.

"No." He loved hearing her voice. A pitch or two lower and it might be called a whiskey voice. It wasn't as rough as that, though. More bourbon cured.

Her movements were quick and precise, without wasted motion, as she flitted from one side of the tree to the other, anchoring bows. "Here." She pulled on one of his arms and draped long ribbons over it. "We're almost ready for the bears."

"Fine." He hopped down from the stepladder. "Have you eaten?" he asked suddenly.

"Mmm."

"Is that a yes or a no?"

"It's an I-had-a-late-lunch-and-I'm-too-busy-and-not-hungry-enough-to-stop."

"I suppose that's a good thing since I don't think there's any food in the kitchen."

Holly shot him an unreadable look. "Typical lawyer behavior."

"Hey," Adam protested. "There are all sorts of people who make a living delivering food to mean old lawyers."

"You don't get out much?"

"No. I flew to Boston for Thanksgiving last week. Other than that, you're the first person I've met outside of the office."

"Business must be good." Holly's voice was muffled as she bent over the mound of bears. "Here, take these for me."

Adam took an armful of bears from her.

"Start hanging those on the back of the tree by the window."

Something flared in Adam's eyes. "Please," Holly added belatedly. "You have to watch me or I'll start treating you like one of my sisters."

Adam raised a black brow. "Not for long, you won't."

Holly watched him negotiate his way behind the tree, turning before he caught her at it.

"What do you think?" she asked a surprisingly short time later, her animated face filled with satisfaction as she checked the tree.

"It's...cute." Adam's half smile neatly displayed an engaging dimple. "Cute but simple. I like simple, but I thought you wanted extraordinary."

Holly sighed. "I do and you're right." She stared at the tree. "I'm not used to changing themes like this. I like to plan in advance." She was silent for a moment, going over her inventory in her mind. "I've got some white-and-silver-glittered snowflakes, and maybe some clear ones. If I had more time..." She looked at him. "I hate to impose—"

"It's no imposition," Adam assured her hastily.

"I was supposed to be finished by now. On the other hand, if I had a chance, I could get to a fabric store tomorrow morning. Silver lamé would make a great tree skirt. I could settle for white batting in a pinch..."

"But you don't want to settle when you could be outstanding."

Holly nodded. "If I could keep the key for another day..."

"Sure." Adam gestured negligently. "Come any time."

"Thanks." Holly ignored the extra invitation she heard in his voice. "May I use the phone?"

"Help yourself."

Holly was already reaching for the telephone when she jerked her hand back. "No, I'm not going to call them." She backed away from the phone clasping her hands together. "My sisters," she explained to Adam. "They're doing another tree and it's the first time I've let them handle a job on their own. I can't call them, or they'll think I don't trust them."

Adam slowly packed the boxes. "How about a toast to a job well done?"

"It's late..."

"But not as late as it would have been if you'd done this all by yourself." Adam smiled persuasively and headed toward the liquor cabinet. "This is bound to be well stocked. Yes," he confirmed, "it is. Now what would you like? White wine, sherry, scotch... bourbon?"

Holly didn't hear him. She had pushed the sleeves of her sweater above her elbows and stuck her hands in the back of her jeans, still studying her Christmas tree.

The room darkened just as Adam reached for a rich old sherry he thought matched Holly's eyes. He made his way toward her avoiding the nearly invisible black Steinway piano, guided only by the flicker of the fire and the twinkle of tiny white Christmas-tree lights.

Holly sat on the floor, leaning against the couch.

"Wishing for a bearskin rug?" Adam asked as he placed the bottle and glasses on the coffee table and sat next to her.

"Oh, Adam! Yes! Do you know where I can get one? I've got an idea, but it's a long shot." In her excitement, Holly grabbed his arm, preventing him from pouring their sherry. "Just think—the perfect touch!"

"No, I—"

"The *Town Square* people will love it. Maybe they'll even use my tree for the cover." Holly hugged her knees to her chest.

Adam felt the potential mood slipping away. "Sherry?"

"Mmm." Holly was still dreaming of magazine covers. "It's good. Exactly right."

Adam shifted closer. "It matches your—"

The jangling of the telephone made them both jump. Adam was already off balance and managed to slosh a few drops of sherry onto his jeans. He looked around for something to dab it up, ignoring the phone.

"Aren't you going to answer it?"

"Why? The only calls on this phone are wrong numbers." Adam headed for the kitchen and a paper towel. "Calls for me come on the private phone line in the bedroom. But go ahead and answer if it bothers you."

"Penthouse," Holly said, wondering if she should add the law firm's lengthy name.

"Holly! There's been a terrible mistake. We're ruined."

"Laurel, calm down. Are you all right? Is Ivy?" Hearing the agitated voice of her normally placid younger sister

upset Holly more than she would have expected. She was
only vaguely aware that Adam had returned.

"No one's hurt—yet. But the sorority is furious. They
said I switched decorations on purpose. I've never been so
humiliated."

Holly took a deep breath. "What happened?" she asked
with a sense of foreboding.

"The Alumnae Christmas Coffee is tomorrow and they
said they picked the teddy-bear theme—you know bears are
our mascot."

"And you've done a lovely Art Deco tree for them."
Holly stared at the white bears—and the brown ones—in
dismay.

"How did you know?"

"I've got the bears."

"Holly, you *can't*," Laurel wailed. "Listen, some of my
friends are here. They brought food by for the coffee. It's
bad enough that they see me working, but they're being so
nasty about everything. The Deco tree is classy."

"But it wasn't what they chose. Is Ivy there with you?"

"Yes."

"Get her to help you strip the tree. I'm on my way with
the teddy bears."

As Holly hung up the phone, she could feel a heavy fa-
tigue settling around her. Her shoulders slumped and she
frowned in disappointment. She had counted on them,
really counted on them.

"That was my sister." Holly gestured to the phone as she
turned to face Adam. He stood leaning against the wall,
arms crossed over his chest. "It appears the design orders
were switched. She has the Art Deco tree your firm must
have ordered." Holly wearily rubbed her temple. "All that
work—"

"Leave it," Adam ordered. "You're done in. I say the
tree is wonderful. It stays as it is."

Holly hesitated, wanting to believe him.

"I heard you tell your sister you were bringing her these other bears. Let's get moving." Adam began loading boxes onto the dolly.

"Thanks for your help." Holly secured the boxes with cords. "I'll try not to wake you when I get back here tomorrow morning to do the tree skirt."

"I'm coming with you now."

"Adam..." It was tempting, really tempting.

"It'll be fun for me and you're too tired to enjoy anything right now." Adam lifted a hand to the base of her neck and kneaded it briefly. Then he swung her gently around and pressed the elevator button.

"No. I'll be fine." Holly shrugged off his hand and wheeled the dolly into the private elevator, realizing she sounded curt. She was tired and she was honestly sorry her younger sisters had botched the orders.

She turned—and saw Adam's expression. A frown had etched faint lines of concern around his mouth. "I'll see you tomorrow," she said to soften her refusal.

"Okay." Adam's smile didn't reach his eyes.

She had to face him until the padded doors whispered shut. She felt horrible. What was the matter with her? He had no business coming along. He was a *client*.

Her fingers hovered over the buttons, then pressed one. The doors opened. "Get in," she relented, "if you still want to come."

Adam did, and he entered the elevator with a blinding smile that temporarily banished all her misgivings.

"You won't regret it, ma'am. I'm an experienced tree decorator."

Holly laughed, feeling lighter and, well, merrier.

"Wait!" Adam stopped her from releasing the button and stuck his head outside the elevator. He gazed at the ceiling, then nodded.

"What are you doing?" Holly asked as the doors slid shut.

Unblinking, he regarded her lips and smiled slowly. "Measuring for mistletoe."

CHAPTER TWO

HOLLY MANEUVERED her dark green van between the parked cars on the crushed-gravel drive and drove to the front of the white plantation-style sorority house. Two familiar figures sat beside a stack of boxes strapped to a dolly like the one in the back of the van.

Holly looked at Adam and sighed. "My sisters." She hopped down to unlock the van's double doors.

"Let me." Adam reached inside for the dolly, his shoulder brushing hers. Startled by the jolt of awareness she felt, Holly quickly backed away. Her sisters provided a welcome distraction.

"I'm *sorry*," Ivy apologized with an aggrieved look at Laurel. It obviously wasn't the first time she'd done so.

"It was humiliating," came Laurel's whiskey-voiced declaration. "And in front of my own sorority sisters. It'll be all over SMU by tomorrow morning. I never wanted to do this in the first place."

Holly quickly intervened before Adam was exposed to any more sisterly squabbling.

"Laurel, it was your idea to approach the sororities, since the students are busy with finals. And it was a good one," she added hastily. "With all the jobs we're doing this season, a mix-up was bound to happen sooner or later," she said, directing a reassuring look at Ivy. "Don't worry about it. I've got the right decorations, but we're going to have to trim the tree now. I know it's late—will it be a problem for the girls to have us working?" she asked Laurel.

But her sisters had noticed Adam. He flashed them a grin as he shut the van's doors. "Hi."

"Hello." They spoke in unison and turned questioning eyes to Holly.

"Adam is a temporary recruit. Adam Markland, my sisters, Laurel and Ivy."

Laurel sidled forward. "I hope you're aware of the honor, Adam. Holly never allows us to have guests on a job."

Every so often, Holly noticed, there was a drop or two of vinegar in Laurel's syrupy voice. "Adam lives in the penthouse that should have had the Art Deco tree. You remember—the one being photographed for *Town Square* tomorrow morning?"

If she hadn't been so tired, she would have been able to keep her own caustic remark to herself. She regretted the words even before Ivy's eyes filled with tears.

"I've ruined everything!"

Holly closed her eyes briefly as she geared herself up for another pep talk. "Are you kidding? This is nothing compared to what we've faced before. Hitches like this are going to happen. We just have to go on. We can make it work—we *have* to—and we will!"

Laurel and Ivy nodded as Holly spoke, responding to a litany they'd heard before.

Another crisis averted. Holly breathed an inward sigh of relief until she stood in the foyer. She came to a sudden halt, lips parted. "Did they steal the White House Christmas tree?"

The beautiful fir in the sorority-house atrium, soared two stories above them.

"We always got one like that when I lived here," Laurel said. Holly's shocked face didn't seem to faze her a bit. "You're worried about the top, aren't you? No problem. See, you can get to it from the balcony."

"I'm worried about the middle." Holly slumped onto the bottom step suddenly feeling very tired.

"I'll start unloading, Holly." Adam's voice sounded just above her.

"Wait. I need to think. We might not use these." Holly stared at the giant tree, elbows on her knees, hands steepled. Adam's hand rested briefly on her shoulder and he sat quietly beside her. The reassuring warmth of his simple touch relaxed the kinks in her upper back.

"Quiet! Genius at work!" came Laurel's snide remark.

"I'm open to suggestions," Holly countered. Couldn't Laurel behave herself just this once? "Even if you'd had the right decorations, there aren't enough for that tree. Didn't you tell them what size to buy?"

"We've always had a big tree here," Laurel said matter-of-factly.

"What did you decorate it with?"

"A mishmash. It never looked very good."

Holly rolled her eyes.

"That's why I was able to persuade them to hire us!"

Holly ran her hands through her curls. "That tree will swallow decorations. It needs more—that's why we charge extra for large trees."

"You always said simple was more elegant, that it was easy to overdo," offered Ivy in a small voice.

"That's not the problem here!" Holly said, her exasperation evident.

Laurel narrowed her eyes. "But you're oh-so-thrilled we had one, right? All evening, Ivy and I wondered when you'd show up."

"You called me," Holly reminded her.

"Just giving Mama hen an excuse to rescue her baby chicks."

"Laurel," Holly warned, acutely aware of Adam beside her. "We're all tired and edgy. Let's just do the best we can."

"If the tree in the penthouse is a sample of your usual work, your best will be more than enough." Adam leaned closer as he spoke, his words caressing both her cheek and her bruised feelings.

Adam had been so terrific, he didn't deserve to be subjected to this. Holly turned to him with a sheepish smile. "We usually get along just fine."

He smiled. "Sure you do. I've got a younger brother and sister myself."

She wrinkled her nose. "But you're not still living with them."

"Holly?" Ivy spoke hesitantly, her hands clasped nervously together.

Adam noted idly that Ivy's voice had the same low pitch as her sisters' and he'd run out of liquor to describe it to himself. Brandy? Holly jumped up and offered him a hand. He found himself grasping it, glad of an excuse to touch her again. He didn't let go, and for the moment, Holly was content to leave her hand in his.

Ivy continued, "If we've got the Deco *and* the bears here, what did you put on Adam's tree?"

Holly looked quickly at Adam and laughed. "Polar bears."

"We don't have them." Laurel began bumping the dolly down the two steps onto the tiled floor of the atrium.

"We do now."

Laurel shot her a shrewd look, which Holly met blandly. "Buy them from Bloomie?"

Holly swallowed. "Uh-huh."

Laurel and Ivy exchanged a glance before unsnapping the cords and opening the boxes.

The four of them stared at the contents of the boxes and then at the tree. "Okay, here's what we'll do," Holly said briskly. "Ivy, go back home and get the ribbons and bows left from that job where the tree was too small. And...don't we have some grapevine wreaths somewhere? Bring *lots* of ribbon. Any color." Holly closed her eyes to the wine-colored furniture in the public areas ringing the atrium. They didn't have time for the nuances of color coordination now.

"I've got it!" Laurel's dramatic declaration caught the group's attention. Holly sneaked a peek at Adam and wistfully saw that he seemed as fascinated with Laurel as every other man who'd met her. Even though she'd long ago accepted Laurel's effect on men, Holly had hoped Adam would be immune. Of course, she hadn't staked her claim or anything. And she knew Laurel wouldn't deliberately steal him—she gave her credit for that.

"You were going to tell us these bears were too small, weren't you, Holly?"

Holly gave her a lopsided grin. "Eventually."

"There are hundreds of teddy bears in this house. They're our mascot, remember? We'll borrow them and put them on the tree. We can use that pretty green plaid ribbon to tie bows around their necks. The unifying theme, right?" Laurel paused to note the group's approval.

Holly opened her mouth, but Laurel rushed on, "I know burgundy ribbon would be better with the furniture, but I don't think we have that much in stock."

Holly began to nod. "It'll work." She grinned at Laurel. "It'll work, don't you think, Adam? It's got to work." She seized his arm, looking up at him eagerly.

"Bear bows?" he asked faintly.

Holly noticed Adam was more enthusiastic about an hour later, when he found himself surrounded by several dozen pajama-clad young women clutching teddy bears.

"I like your job," he said to Holly as she whirled past him. "I'll bet," she replied, raising her brows at the line of nymphettes waiting to have Adam add ribbons to their bears. She hadn't missed the fact that when the girls returned upstairs to sort through their stuffed animals, many had exchanged voluminous football jerseys and ratty bathrobes for teddies of quite a different sort.

She could hardly blame them, she thought as she once again pushed the sleeves of her oversize sweater above her elbows. Adam had charm. He was older and had an innate sophistication guaranteed to appeal to the college women. And to her.

The tree-decorating turned into a party. No one had been asleep, even though it was approaching midnight. And clearly, no one had any intention of going to sleep now. Adam was definitely enjoying himself.

"I've got no right to be jealous. I've got no *time* to be jealous," Holly said softly to herself. They'd only just met, but she couldn't stop reminiscing about the quiet conversation in front of the fire, or stifle the tingle of anticipation she felt at the thought of seeing him tomorrow.

She was glad Adam had come with them, she realized, watching as he deftly fastened the bears to the branches in the middle of the tree. Not that she wouldn't have been able to handle it herself. She'd always managed before, and she wasn't about to go all mushy and helpless over an attractive man.

Of course, Adam's looks transcended mere attractiveness.

"Do you think we can get him to come with us to do all the other sororities' trees?"

"Laurel! You didn't tell me. That's fantastic—"

"Oh, we don't have them as clients yet," Laurel said confidently, "but we will. Just wait until word gets out about this."

"I think it already has." Holly motioned toward the disapproving housemother who had appeared on the scene.

"Never mind, this will make our reputation," Laurel said. "I guarantee they'll be talking about the Epsilon Eta girls for weeks."

"I thought you meant Deck the Halls's reputation."

"I did, but there *are* other things in life, as I hope you've finally noticed," Laurel replied with a nod upward at Adam.

Holly turned her direct gaze on Laurel. "I noticed." She chose another bear to hand up to Adam. "But right now, nothing can interfere with Deck the Halls. Nothing."

"A LAWYER? A bankruptcy lawyer?" Ivy looked at Holly in astonished surprise. Her sisters had fired the expected questions at Holly the moment they'd dropped Adam off at the penthouse. She had carefully sidestepped his occupation until now, though she didn't know why she'd bothered. After tomorrow, she wouldn't see him again. She couldn't.

"You made friends with one of those parasites?" Laurel looked at Holly as if she had betrayed national secrets.

"You mean vultures," Ivy corrected.

"What's the difference? Both feed off dead bodies," Laurel said caustically.

"Or dead companies," Ivy added with bitterness.

Holly felt relieved. Ivy and Laurel were helping her feel the anger and resolve Adam had dazzled out of her. He'd caught her at a weak moment, that was all.

She unlocked the front door to a home not much smaller than the sorority house they'd just left. "I'm glad you two didn't let your feelings show around Adam. It would be a novelty to have a lawyer on our side." Holly propped the door open with a box filled with odds and ends.

"We didn't know he was a lawyer then," Ivy reminded her.

"He could have made things very difficult. I was supposed to be finished and out of that penthouse by ten. I wasn't and had the wrong decorations to boot."

"Ah, yes. Bloomie to your rescue." Laurel rolled the dolly out of the van.

"Where's Mama's necklace going this time?" Ivy slammed the van doors shut so that Holly could drive it around to the garage.

"Ruthie's wedding." It was difficult to meet Ivy's eyes.

"I wondered why she hadn't been working in their shop lately. Well, you better hope Bloomie doesn't dance with any jewelers," Ivy warned.

"Now that has possibilities," said Laurel, who'd returned for the second cart. "We could claim the real necklace was stolen. Is it still insured Holly?"

Holly shook her head as she started the van. "Too expensive. Mama only kept the policy so that Daddy wouldn't know she'd sold the real diamonds."

"Sure explains how she stretched the household money." Laurel dropped the last of the boxes with a soft thud. "I'm pooped. Let's unpack in the morning."

"It's already morning," Ivy said, heading for the stairs just as Holly came down the hall.

"Ladies, sleep will have to wait." Holly raised her voice to drown out the inevitable moaning. "The photo shoot at the penthouse begins at ten and that tree needs more more work. Ivy, why don't you look for those silver snowflakes? I've got some stuff I'd like to take over just in case they want some of the room decorated. You ought to see it, the Art Deco would have been—" Holly broke off and hoped Ivy wouldn't get upset all over again.

"Laurel, if you really think the other sororities would be interested, you should take the portfolio around tomorrow morning. We need to update our supply list so that we don't have any more mix-ups. After that, you can pack for the Stoffer's job. I've got two trees there. What do you think about doing an angel tree and the Deco one, now that the stuff's available?''

"I don't think. I can't think. I'm exhausted." Laurel pressed her hands to her head. "Holly, the main season's only a week old and look at us. We can't keep this up."

"We have to," Holly said grimly. "Look, we're so close to making Deck the Halls support us for the whole year. You don't want to go back to Exemplary Temporaries any more than I do."

Laurel brushed her lightened, champagne-streaked hair back from her face. "Lord, I hate that place. Still can't pronounce it, but right now, it's looking better and better." She turned to go up the stairs, nearly tripping over a warm, inanimate object.

Ivy had fallen asleep, her head against the railing.

Laurel glared reproachfully at Holly. "It can wait until morning. Come on, Ivy."

Holly grabbed her arm. "The *Town Square* shoot is the biggest break we've ever had! If we play it right, we could have more clients than we can handle." Holly watched in vexation as Laurel ignored her, helping a groggy Ivy to her feet.

"Gotta get snowflakes for Holly," Ivy mumbled.

"Later," Laurel murmured to her. "She's exhausted, Holly!"

"We might get the *cover*. Don't you understand how important this is? You can sleep all afternoon!" Holly argued.

"I want to sleep now," Laurel said, each word distinct and final. "Tomorrow afternoon, you'll have something else for us to do."

"You're right," Holly said, making it sound like an accusation. "You two get some sleep. I'll come upstairs in a little while."

"Lay off, Holly. You can stay down here and play martyr by yourself this time." Laurel continued to guide Ivy up the stairs. "Besides, the Stoffer job is for charity and it's stupid to waste our two best themes on them."

Holly stared at her sisters and blinked rapidly. If they'd just work a little harder. That wasn't too much to ask. It wasn't as though it would be forever—just during the Christmas season.

She'd make it in spite of them. In spite of everyone. Holly ran her fingers through her curls and rubbed her neck and shoulders. She ached to follow Ivy and Laurel up the stairs.

The chirp of the telephone on the hall table startled her and she jerked up the receiver before the second ring. Who would call at two o'clock in the morning? Holly was tempted to hang up, convinced it must be a crank call. On the other hand, didn't relatives always call with bad news in the middle of the night? Memories of another middle-of-the-night phone call haunted her as she spoke softly into the receiver.

"Come have breakfast with me." The pleasant, honey-coated words instantly soothed her apprehensions.

"Adam." Holly closed her eyes and allowed her smile to sound in her voice.

"I'll cook."

"That's quite an offer."

"Is that a yes?"

The almost whispered words wrapped Holly in a sensation of warm intimacy as she stood in the dark hall.

"Yes."

"Sweet dreams."

Holly smiled and gently put the receiver down. Adam's words were a good-night caress. Had she already been in bed, she could have fallen asleep with their echoes. The thought was very appealing.

But not as appealing as a *Town Square* magazine cover.

Holly started walking briskly toward the laundry, hoping the plastic snowflakes were stored in what had once been the maid's quarters.

HOLLY HAD NEVER REALIZED how heavy a polar-bear rug could be. She enveloped herself in its musty warmth and leaned against the padded walls of the elevator, oblivious to the white hairs that rubbed off.

"I don't believe it." Adam shook his head as the private elevator opened and Holly and the bear emerged. "Where did you get that thing?"

"From the display window at a travel agency. They were promoting ski trips." Holly lurched over to the fireplace, heaved the bear off her shoulders and arranged it in front of the white-brick hearth. "Her name is Bianca."

"They just let you walk out with it—her? Or did you and your sisters do a little breaking and entering after you dropped me off?"

Holly's angry reaction caught Adam unprepared.

"We don't break the law." She gazed at him with a disturbingly intent look. It willed him to believe her.

The twinkle, usually present in Adam's blue eyes, was momentarily extinguished and his face became a pleasantly bland mask. Yet its mildness was purposeful and controlled. "I'm not implying that you do," he said in a voice that matched his expression. "I meant it as a joke."

Holly guessed this was his courtroom face, even though he'd denied that he spent time in the courtroom. It just seemed to be something lawyers knew how to do.

"Furthermore, I resent this unfounded hostility you have toward me. I was not involved in whatever legal problems you've had in the past, and I'm tired of tiptoeing around in case I step on your feelings.'' Adam stood above her, his face devoid of the warmth she'd come to expect.

Holly's lips parted slightly. She missed his smile with its outrageous dimples. "What was the question?"

"You three do a little breaking and entering after you dropped me off?" Adam repeated lightly.

"Nah. Would have been easier. One of us has to go back and redecorate their window."

Holly was wrestling with the bear and missed the look of tenderness on Adam's face. She looked particularly soft and touchable this morning. She wore camel-colored slacks and a creamy turtleneck sweater, and had negligently cast off a matching tan coat, which had slid from the sofa to the floor.

As Adam bent to pick it up, he noted the label and felt the extravagant softness that told him it was camel hair.

Holly was on her knees, turning the bear this way and that. Adam silently placed the coat on the sofa, next to the shoulder bag Holly had slung down beside it. A rich brown alligator. He shoved his hands into his pockets and checked her shoes. Matching loafers.

Adam began to piece together Holly's unmentioned past. Last night's visit to the private and expensive Southern Methodist University campus, accompanied by Laurel's references to her sorority, told him Holly and her sisters had come from a privileged background.

No wonder she was so defensive. He longed to tell her she wasn't alone. He'd seen plenty of Texas oil barons who had fallen on hard times.

"Mmm, is that breakfast I smell? Coffee in particular?"

"Uh, yes." Adam found it difficult to switch gears. "But that coffee has been sitting since six-thirty."

"That's only an hour and a half. It'll be great." Holly had preceded him into the kitchen and emptied the pot into two waiting mugs. She automatically removed the grounds and began to measure out more for another pot.

"I'll do that."

"Good." She relinquished the pot without argument. "I have a confession. I've already been here this morning and I left some boxes downstairs with the security guard. The travel agency wasn't supposed to open until nine, but I talked them into coming in early."

She was pleased with herself and had a right to be, she thought. How many cruises had that same agency arranged for her parents when they were alive? And the European "Grand Tour" she and Laurel had each taken the summer they turned nineteen—but Ivy couldn't. It was a favor for old time's sake.

"Better make a large pot," Holly said as she scanned the refrigerator for milk or cream. "I was up until four this morning." She found a white liquid in a cream pitcher, sniffed it and poured a generous amount into her coffee.

"Ah." She took a sizable swallow. "It's good. I'm glad you don't make wimpy coffee. I can't stand wimpy coffee." She drained her cup.

Adam glanced at her and added two more tablespoons of grounds to the filter basket.

"I'll be right back." Holly smiled breezily at him.

"I'll help you."

His eyes were even bluer this morning than they'd been last night. "Making the coffee is help enough."

When the elevator doors opened to the penthouse again, Holly had no trouble convincing herself to abandon the boxes and follow her nose to the source of the wonderful smells.

Adam heard her and had a cup of the milky coffee she liked ready for her.

"I could get spoiled," she sighed as she leaned against the doorway to the kitchen. "I see we're dining in state." She nodded toward the settings on the smoked-glass top of the dining-room table.

"No room in the kitchen." Adam handed her a bowl of strawberries.

"How decadent," Holly said before popping one into her mouth. "Strawberries in December."

"Imported from New Zealand. I got there just as they were unloading them."

"Got where? New Zealand?"

"I might have. For you." He met her eyes briefly before turning back to the stove. "As it was, I stopped by an all-night gourmet grocery not too far from here."

The only all-night gourmet grocery in Dallas was twenty miles away. Holly set the bowl on the table with hands that suddenly shook. Caffeine jitters, obviously—and not the disturbing intimacy of sharing breakfast with an attractive man she hardly knew. In fact, it felt perfectly natural to be here for breakfast. *That* was what concerned her.

"Eggs Benedict?" Holly watched as Adam carried in the plates and presented them with a flourish. "We'll have to do this more often." The remark just popped out and in less than a heartbeat, Holly realized exactly how Adam was going to interpret it.

His black brow raised; a half smile deepened a dimple. "Certainly."

Holly clutched her fork, determined to ignore all innuendos. It wouldn't be fair to flirt with him now. "I'm impressed. But does it taste as good as it looks?" With Adam watching closely, she took a bite, resolving to be complimentary even if it tasted like sawdust. At this point, she didn't trust herself to notice the difference anyway.

"I don't cook often," he warned.

Holly rolled her eyes and took another mouthful. "It's wonderful. Beginner's luck."

When Adam returned to the kitchen for more coffee, he tossed the empty jar of ready-made hollandaise sauce into the trash.

Holly nearly collided with him as she brought the dishes into the kitchen. "Do you have time for more coffee? Don't you have to get to work?"

"People can manage without me for a couple of hours."

Glancing at her watch, Holly wiped her mouth on a napkin. "Good. I want to help with the dishes, but it's nearly nine and I've got to get to a fabric store. Gus—he's the photographer—and the magazine people will come about ten. They had another shoot before this one. I'll probably have to beat on the shop doors, but I'm determined to have silver lamé for this tree."

Holly kept up her nervous chatter as she shrugged into her coat and grabbed her purse. "Thanks for breakfast. And please, if you have to leave before I get back, dump the dishes in the sink and I'll finish cleaning up later." She punched the elevator button.

"I thought I'd stick around and watch." The quiet words silenced her as she stepped inside the elevator.

The doors had already begun to close. Holly jabbed her foot between them and they shuddered apart. The look on Adam's face might have been the beginning of a smile. The sleeves of his crisp white shirt were rolled to the elbows, revealing the fine black hair on his arms, and he had a dish towel tucked in the waistband of dark charcoal pants. He still held the coffeepot, like a husband seeing his wife off to work just before he left for his own office.

A tiny lock of blue-black hair separated itself from the rest of the smooth wave across his forehead and Holly longed to push it back into place.

He'd be too distracting. She didn't dare allow him to stay, so this was goodbye. Even if he wanted to see her again, the timing was incredibly awful.

The profits Holly and her sisters made in December determined their standard of living for the next year. She was too busy to nurture a beginning relationship, never mind that he was a lawyer. Even when she'd first admired his appealing dimples and the brilliant laser-blue eyes, she had known the timing was wrong and would be for years.

Holly's lips were parted as she stared at him. Neither one had said goodbye. She took a deep breath; she was going to have to say it first. "I enjoyed breakfast. A lot. But..." Did he have to be so gorgeous?

The telephone rang. They glanced at it and at each other. "Here, hold this." Adam yanked her out of the elevator and handed her the coffeepot, then sprinted for the phone. Holly tried to convince herself to carry the pot back to the kitchen and quietly make her getaway. Her feet were fused to the Italian marble floor of the entry.

"Yes, Laurel, she's here." Adam waved an arm in her direction. "For you."

She set the coffeepot on the floor and practically flew to the phone.

"Holly? Do you have the fabric yet?"

"I was just on my way."

"Great. I'll be right up. You'll love this."

Holly turned to Adam as she replaced the receiver. "She's on her way up."

Adam walked over to the coffeepot she had left in front of the elevator. "Good. There's just enough for three more cups."

Holly grinned. It hadn't taken him long to figure out her vice. Off came her camel coat. She really did like Adam, she decided, even if he was a lawyer. What rotten luck.

"Not bad." Laurel entered the penthouse, looking first at the tree, then at Adam, who was bringing a third cup of coffee. "So you weren't a mirage." She took the mug from Adam and presented a Neiman-Marcus shopping bag to Holly. "See what you think of this."

Holly pulled out a long slink of a dress in silver lamé. "Laurel, are you sure?"

"I've got no place to wear it and you need the time." She sipped her coffee as Holly arranged the dress under the tree. "Here, stuff it with this." Laurel began to wad the tissue paper she'd packed in the bottom of the shopping bag.

"Thanks, Laurel. You're a lifesaver." The sisters exchanged a long look filled with understanding.

"I have my moments. What have you two been doing? I don't see any snowflakes."

Adam began opening the boxes Holly had brought earlier.

"You don't have to do that, Adam. Laurel can help."

"No, Laurel can't. I'm off to the Alumnae Christmas Coffee. I just stopped by here to deliver the dress—excuse me, tree skirt."

Holly sat back on her heels. Laurel's red silk dress and the sisters' communal fur jacket registered at last. How could she think of going to a party when they had so much to do?

Laurel correctly read Holly's look. "I *was* invited to the Alumnae Christmas Coffee." She dangled a camera from her fingers. "I thought I'd go early and get some pictures for our portfolio, since Gus will be here."

"You're right." Holly offered a smile in apology.

Laurel bent down and ruffled her sister's curls. "It's okay. I left Ivy at home waiting for Mrs. Bloom."

"Oh, no! I completely forgot about Bloomie."

"You've got enough on your mind." Laurel slanted a glance at Adam and mouthed, "He's okay for a lawyer."

Holly nodded, with a wistful look over her shoulder as they walked toward the elevator.

"I'll be late getting back. I volunteered to be on the clean-up committee." Laurel adjusted her purse so it wouldn't crush the fur.

"Whatever for?"

"Leftovers," Laurel said succinctly.

"Good thinking."

"I told you I can think better when I've had some sleep. Just imagine what I could do with a whole night!"

Adam was on the telephone when Holly returned to the tree. "I need to go into the office," he said, rolling down his sleeves. He passed by Holly and disappeared into a bedroom, reappearing as the consummate lawyer, complete with briefcase. "I'll try to get back here for lunch. How about deli food and leftover strawberries?"

Holly's fingers raked her hair in the familiar gesture. "Adam, please don't go to all this trouble. I don't even know if I'll still be here." It was frightening to see how effortlessly he fit into her life, overscheduled though it was. She'd already caught herself mentally depending on him and she'd known him for less than a day. How could she allow herself to forget that the only person she could depend on was herself?

"I'll call first." He waved a hand as the elevator doors shut. "Relax for once."

Holly smiled to herself. He hadn't said goodbye.

CHAPTER THREE

HOLLY FINISHED THE TREE, added Christmasy touches to the general vicinity and decided to take Adam's advice. Who knew when she'd get another chance to relax?

Maybe next year Deck the Halls could hire some part-time help or sales staff. It would depend on whether the exposure from this layout resulted in more jobs. A *lot* more jobs.

In theory, Holly and her sisters lived year-round on the profits from the Christmas season. In reality, they usually ran out of money by the summer and worked as temporary office personnel for a few months. Holly counted progress in terms of when they had to call Exemplary Temporaries. This year, they'd made it all the way to August. Of course, Holly wasn't about to let them come close to going broke. So they'd been working as temps since March.

Next year would be different. It would take only a few more jobs now to squeeze in September's and October's expenses before they began full-time preparations again in November. She'd have to be firmer with Adam. She literally couldn't afford to get involved.

Holly closed her eyes and thought of her parents. This would be the fifth Christmas without them. Five Christmases of struggle. Why did it have to be such work?

The faint click of a shutter startled her into wakefulness.

"Great! I'll call it Christmas Beauty. I could sell it like that." The man with the camera snapped his fingers. "Make your fortune, babe. And the less you wear, the more you make."

Holly straightened on the sofa. "Gus, the only thing that's going to get exposed around here is film."

"I think I'll call it Christmas Cactus."

"I won't sign the model release."

He shrugged. "Pity."

People poured out of the elevator, dragging lighting equipment and extension cords.

"What time is it?" Holly still felt bleary-eyed from her interrupted nap.

"'Bout ten-thirty, give or take a few."

"Ugh." Holly shook her head slightly. "You look like I feel."

Gus grinned down at his fraying jeans and worn plaid shirt. "I'm workin'." He tossed back long, lank hair and rubbed his scraggly beard. "Didn't get around to shaving this morning."

"Or any other morning."

Gus shrugged his thin shoulders.

"I brought some extra stuff, in case you need to do some wide-angle shots. Who's in charge? Will you introduce me?" Holly studied the half dozen people in the *Town Square* entourage.

Gus pointed to a striking brunette in skinny black pants topped by a tunic sweater, then turned away to consult with one of the technicians.

"That's it?" she exclaimed in an accusing undertone. "You promised a lot of contacts."

"Look, babe, I opened the door. You gotta walk through."

With a look of exasperation, she thought of Gus's unabashed seediness and decided she might do better on her own.

"Hello, I'm Holly Hall," she said, approaching the brunette.

"Beth Robinson, with *Town Square*. Are you Swinehart, Cathardy and Steele's representative?"

"No, but they hired my firm to do the decorating. Let me give you my card."

The other woman nodded as she glanced at it. "The tree's unexpected, but I like it. It adds a touch of whimsy. I'll admit I'm rather surprised at the firm's choice. They have such a . . . formidable reputation."

"Yes." Holly smiled widely, frantically trying to think of something to say.

"I suppose the rug gave you the idea for the theme." Beth Robinson made notes on a clipboard.

Holly miserably wondered if Beth would put that in the accompanying article. It should have occurred to her before now that the law firm might object to the change in decorations. But Adam had told her the tree was great, hadn't he?

"Um, not—"

"Beth!"

She smiled dismissively at Holly and walked over to a man positioning umbrella reflectors.

"Classy place. Funky tree." Gus appeared beside her, taking light readings. "Weird choice."

"Gus," Holly said through clenched teeth and a broad smile. "There was a slight miscommunication, but everything's fine now. Did you spread the word that Deck the Halls has a few openings left this season?"

Gus smirked. "Only a few?"

"The tree's over here."

"I know." Gus crouched down, glanced impatiently at the white light from the windows and took some readings of the fireplace. "Holly, go stand over there, will ya?"

She complied, wishing the fireplace had a mantel and that she'd decorated it, since Gus seemed to find it so fascinating.

"Sit."

Holly sat.

"No." Gus waved her down. "On the rug. I see ashes, so the thing works, right? But you probably wouldn't know."

Holly stared at the telltale ashes, remembering. Half-smiling, she carefully unwrapped her memories of Adam: images of dimples, a bewitching cleft in his chin, and blue, blue eyes. She felt again the warmth radiating from the fireplace and saw the glimmer of crystal catching the light.

"Okay, thanks, babe."

Holly nodded at Gus. Before she got out of the way, she took the brush from the tools by the fireplace and swept the coating of fine powdery ashes from the white brick. It was an unusual fireplace set. Holly positioned the tools so the engraved logo of the law firm was visible and would get into the photographs of the tree. The name would add prestige to her portfolio.

WHY COULDN'T THE GUY have stayed hidden one more day? Of all the times for there to be a break in the embezzlement case... Adam loosened an already loose tie and waved the courier into his office. Simultaneously dictating information into the phone, he thrust a sheaf of papers into a nine-by-twelve envelope, scrawled a name and address on the outside and handed it to the waiting teenager.

With his now free hand, Adam plugged his ear, trying to concentrate on the tinny bureaucratic voice at the other end of the line. A few feet away, Bernard Steele, of Swinehart, Cathardy and Steele, spoke into the other telephone in Adam's office.

Hanging up the phone, Adam glanced at his watch, surprised to find that it was only ten-thirty. He wondered how Holly was getting along with the photographers.

"Do you think we can get those extradition papers in time? Joe's booked on the next three flights to Mexico City." The older man turned weary eyes toward Adam.

"It'll be close."

"Yeah." The other man stared at nothing. "I suppose it would be too much to hope for that lowlife to stay put. His embezzling might cost a good friend of mine his company." He sighed, then smiled. "Next time you talk to your dad, thank him for letting you go."

"I'll convey your greetings," Adam said after a moment, "but it was my decision to come here."

"Must have been a tough one—you being the first Markland to leave the family firm. 'Course, you have a different style."

Adam's blue eyes gave nothing away. "We weren't getting too many bankruptcy cases." He stood, but Mr. Steele showed no inclination to leave.

"Not enough for two of you? Isn't it also your sister's field?"

The expression on Adam's face warned Mr. Steele that this had better be the last question about the Marklands. "We each have our preferences. Hers is real-estate law—she likes the hours better now that she has children."

Mr. Steele nodded. "Children." His knees creaked audibly as he struggled from the small sofa. "You never know how they're going to turn out." He sighed again and faced the window. "I feel responsible, you know."

Adam glanced at his watch. He wanted to call Holly before she left. "Pardon?"

"How old are you now, Adam? Twenty-nine? Thirty?"

Adam reached for some papers he didn't want and sat down again. "Thirty-one."

"Eh?" Mr. Steele turned from the window to look at him. "I guess you've turned out all right, then. So far." He faced the window again. "Our embezzler is a friend's son like you.

Younger, though. I recommended him for his job. Supposed to be a financial whiz, by reputation. Didn't really know him, though any son of..."

Mr. Steele lapsed into silence and Adam stifled his impatience.

"None of that matters now." The man by the window couldn't see Adam's irritation. "He betrayed a trust and shamed his daddy and we're gonna get him."

Adam didn't doubt it as he watched the wistful old man become the shrewd and ruthlessly razor-sharp lawyer the world knew.

"In my time a man's handshake was binding and he stood by his word. It's time we brought those days back."

Adam censored a cynical thought. "If we did, we'd all be out of a job," he remarked lightly.

"Not you, Adam. Now, I don't know what differences you and your people had and I don't care." Adam couldn't tell whether Mr. Steele had deliberately misunderstood or not. "I need people I can trust. They're rare, they're rare. But—" he whirled from the window, shattering his pensive mood "—a firm is its reputation. Without that, you have nothing."

Adam picked up his suit jacket and walked Mr. Steele to the door. "Speaking of reputations, it's time I got back to oversee things at the penthouse."

Mr. Steele blinked. "Is there something I've forgotten?"

"The photographers?" Adam prompted.

"Ah." Mr. Steele took a deep breath. "That's today, is it? Well, damn. We'll have to cancel."

Adam caught his breath. Holly would be devastated. He couldn't let that happen. "It may be too late. The photographers are already there. The tree is ready."

"We can't have them running all over the penthouse."

"I agree. I'll be back as soon as I can." Adam opened the door of his office for Mr. Steele.

"The timing on those extradition papers is critical. One of us needs to be here." Neither man moved. "And I'll be in court."

Adam felt a surge of anger. The old man was testing him. This recent bit of nastiness must have affected him more than Adam had realized. He faced Mr. Steele's watery-blue unwavering stare, magnified by thick glasses, and thought of Holly's warm brown eyes. "Canceling and throwing the magazine people out after they've already got there is going to get you some bad press," he pointed out.

Mr. Steele winced. "Just what I was trying to avoid in the first place."

"I'll contact the decorator and have her oversee them." If he couldn't see Holly for lunch, at least he could save the shoot for her.

Mr. Steele's hand crept into a pocket of his baggy pants. "That'd work, I suppose. Tree look good?"

Adam nodded, remembering the mix-up. "It's... approachable. Friendly." He sat at his desk again, his mouth curved in a determined smile.

"Good, good. We're trying to soften our image a little. People seem to think we're too formidable and aloof." Mr. Steele shook his head as if wondering how such strange ideas got started. "Clients have been afraid their cases weren't important enough for us. Get too many people thinking that way and you won't have any clients at all."

Adam smiled, a real smile this time. "Yes, sir, it's a friendly tree, all right."

"Good, good. Doug Hall's gal did it. Got herself quite a little business. Would have made her daddy proud, even if she is a female child. He had all girls. Never seemed to bother him."

Mr. Steele pursed his lips in thought. "His death was a real tragedy."

Adam, who had been about to dial the penthouse, glanced up. "I don't know the story."

"Had some dealings with Doug Hall, like a lot of folks." The old lawyer jabbed a finger at Adam. "Now there was a man who did business by handshake." Some of the vigor left him. "And shouldn't have."

"What happened?" The leather chair sighed as Adam leaned back.

"Douglas Hall and his wife were killed in a light-plane crash on their way to an oil-well fire about four or five years ago. Worst possible time." Mr. Steele shook his head. "He was overextended and the oil recession was on. His affairs were a legal nightmare—or fantasy, depending on your scruples. Some of it's still in litigation. There was nothing left for the girls, but that oldest one wouldn't give up. I felt real bad when she came to me. I had dealings with other parties in the case and frankly, there was no money there. No trust fund—Doug Hall didn't have anything to put in one."

Adam began to get a horribly clear picture of Holly's experiences with lawyers—and with this firm. "Lots of publicity?"

"Oh, my, yes. There was the insurance suit and the fraud thing—some said he set fire to his own well. Nothing was proven, and it's still on appeal."

No wonder Holly hated lawyers. He'd just have to make her change her mind. "I'll give her a call then—since you know the family and you want the publicity."

Mr. Steele studied Adam for a moment and nodded slowly. "That'll be fine, Adam. We can trust Doug Hall's girl to keep an eye on things."

"PHONE'S RINGING." Gus dropped the light meter that dangled from his neck and glanced over his shoulder at the softly purring telephone less than two feet from Holly.

Holly fussed with a bowl of silver and red balls she had brought for the coffee table. "I know." She supposed she had as much right as anyone there to answer the telephone. She tried to make her "hello" sound authoritative.

"Holly? It's Adam. Photographers there yet?"

"Yes." Even with all the commotion, she had instantly recognized his voice.

"I can't get back for our lunch." His voice vibrated with genuine regret and she found it matched her own. "Listen, Mr. Steele wants someone there to supervise, or he'll cancel. I told him you could. Do you have time?"

She'd planned on staying during the actual shoot, anyway. It was nice to know she was now there in an official capacity. "Thanks. It'll be tight but I'll stick around till everyone leaves."

"Good. Can you squeeze in dinner tonight?"

The silence on the phone line was the only silence in the room.

"Holly, move! You're in the way." Gus waved her aside, but the phone cord didn't stretch behind the lights and her shadow was in the picture.

"Adam, let me go to the kitchen phone." She handed the white receiver to Gus. "Hang this up for me?"

"Okay, Gus!" she called when she reached the kitchen. The few moments had given her time to subdue the emotional rush she felt and put Adam's dinner invitation into perspective. He was obviously attracted to her and goodness knew, she was attracted to him. But putting him on hold on the telephone was radically different from putting him on hold in her life. It was better not to start anything; her life was in balance right now—just barely. One more commitment would tip it over.

"Adam . . ."

"You're going to say no. Don't." His voice was quietly compelling.

She leaned her forehead against the cool white tile in the kitchen. "Adam, I can't. I really can't tonight, but even if I could, I shouldn't."

"Holly, Mr. Steele told me about your parents. I'm sorry, but don't turn me down because I'm a lawyer. I want a chance to prove that not all lawyers are alike."

"You've already done that," Holly said. "That's why it's so difficult to say no."

"You've got to eat. I've got to eat."

He wasn't making this easy for her. "That's right, and tonight I'm eating sandwiches in a furniture store. I've got two trees to do." *And all these breakfast dishes,* she thought as she surveyed the monument to their meal. She added a mental reminder and wondered where she'd steal the time to check the boxes of decorations Ivy had packed for tonight.

"Fine," he said easily. "I'll bring the sandwiches and a few other goodies and meet you there. What time?"

"Adam..." Holly sighed in frustration.

"We've established the fact that we're both going to eat. I'm merely proposing that we do it together." He paused while she absorbed that piece of logic. "I've had too many lonely meals lately."

The rat. He was pulling every emotional string she had. "As long as you understand the ground rules," she said firmly, planning to review them herself.

"Sure," he agreed. "I get to work while I eat."

Holly laughed. "You're incorrigible."

"Absolutely," he said in a voice that sent chills down her spine as it warmed her heart. Her resolve had wavered and they both knew it.

"What furniture store?" he asked in the same persuasive voice he'd used during their entire conversation.

This was it. Holly closed her eyes. Decision time. "It'll be a late night," she stalled, hoping she wouldn't have to turn him down again. Knowing she couldn't.

"I do my best work at night."

Her lips quivered. "Stoffer's near Central Expressway. Six o'clock."

And this would be the absolute last time she could see him. It had to be.

"Haven't you started yet?" Holly asked Gus as she returned to the living area.

"Uh, had some trouble finding enough outlets." Gus faced her, but his eyes didn't meet hers.

"Didn't you bring extension cords?" She looked pointedly at her watch. "You're already an hour behind schedule, aren't you?"

"That's my problem," Gus sniffed, fiddling with his camera.

"It's mine, too. That was the law firm on the phone and they want me to stay until you're finished."

This time Gus's eyes did meet hers. "Good. I've got a favor to ask. Stick around."

Whatever she thought of him as a human being, Gus was a superb photographer, Holly marveled as she watched him work. She felt really good about things for once. Gus photographed from all possible angles, with Holly watching from the sidelines. Beth Robinson and her crew had taken over the penthouse. Holly didn't object. For one thing, she didn't want to sabotage her chance at landing this design on the cover of the weekly magazine, and for another, Beth had a good eye.

While the crew loaded the elevator after the shoot, Gus tracked her down in the small kitchen. "How's about you and me teaming up for a little something on the side?"

"Gus, why is it that you can make what is probably a very reasonable request sound lewd and suggestive?" Holly shook her head as she loaded the dishwasher.

Gus grinned and slouched against the doorjamb. "Just keeping all my options open. Which," he continued, "is what I wanted to discuss with you." He looked down at the cameras slung around his neck. "I'd like to take some more photographs."

Holly gestured through the dining area into the living room. "Go ahead."

"Not now." Gus squinted his eyes. "We're running late..."

"And you thought that your old buddy Holly would let you skimp here so you wouldn't be so late to your next appointment." She gave him a disgusted look. "Thanks a lot."

There was a brief flicker of something in Gus's expression. "No, no. You've got it wrong. You know how I am. All these people." He shrugged. "I like working alone."

"What do you want from me?" Holly gave him a hard stare and began wiping the white-tiled counters.

Gus shifted and fiddled with his light meter. "Look, I want some night shots. This place would be great, and there's a bonus if I land the cover. I want you to make sure that the guy who's living here stays away for a while tonight."

"You listened on the extension!"

"So?" He took in her outraged expression and gave her a little shake. "Come on, I'm trying to do you a favor—"

"With a tidy profit for yourself," Holly interjected.

"—and I get shot down. What happened to Holly the Hustler? This might be the cover. Can't you just see it?"

Holly could, and had a thousand times. "I've got to clear it with Adam," she said, ignoring his crack. She dug the key out of her purse and dropped it into his slightly grimy hand. "If he says no, then leave the key with the security guard. Where can I reach you if it's not okay?"

"You can't. Keep him outta here until ten."

"Wait a minute—"

"Thanks, Holly!" Gus ran for the elevator.

"DRAT!" SHE'D FORGOTTEN all about Gus's request to return to the penthouse, Holly realized in the middle of unpacking her angel tree decorations. It had slipped her mind in the rush. Maybe there was still time to alert the guard. Holly stared at her watch, then buried her fingers in her curls. Adam would have left his office by now.

"Hello."

She jumped. "Adam, you startled me."

He looked around at the dozens of people working on their various trees in the mock living rooms. The sounds of crushed tissue paper as ornaments were unwrapped, the scrape of boxes, the squeak of Styrofoam and an occasional tinkle of breaking glass surrounded them. He smiled quizzically. "I did?"

"I was thinking."

"About me, I hope." He knelt quickly and placed a rattan basket before her. "Dinner, as promised."

"In a hamper?" Holly smiled delightedly. "Just like in the movies."

"Of course, just like in the movies. Where do you think I got the idea?" he admitted unselfconsciously.

It was so elegant that Holly felt guiltier than ever.

"How did everything go this morning?" Adam began to unpack the basket and Holly caught the whiff of fresh bread.

"Fine," she chirped, feeling miserable.

"Did they like the tree?" Adam turned one of her boxes into an impromptu table as he covered it with a small cloth.

"I think so." She swallowed. "The photographer told me that he'd like to go back for some night shots. I meant to ask you. Do you mind?"

"When?"

"Tonight? I lent him the key." Holly bit her lip.

Adam studied her for a moment. "Will a lot of people be with him?"

Holly was relieved she could tell Adam no. "He said he'd be working alone."

Adam shrugged. "You obviously trust him, so it shouldn't be a problem."

"Gus is all right." Her eyes brightened. "That tree looks so good against the night skyline, we think they'll use it for the cover shot. It's becoming one of my favorites."

"Mine, too." His eyes held hers.

It was getting more and more difficult to remember that she didn't want a relationship with anyone. "What have you brought to eat? I'm starved," she said quickly, trying to ignore the moment they'd just shared.

"You didn't eat lunch, did you?"

Holly shook her head.

"I was afraid of that. How do you propose to get the energy to keep up this hectic pace you've set for yourself if you don't eat?" Adam set a poor-boy sandwich in front of her and opened a plastic container of crudités.

"Someone special fixed a marvelous breakfast for me." Her voice was soft and huskier than usual.

When she saw the expression on Adam's face, she was almost sorry she'd spoken. It wasn't fair to encourage him.

"The competition is gaining." Adam gestured to the trees taking shape next to them.

"It's okay. As a pro, I'm disqualified. This is all for charity. Different organizations decorate trees and the public votes on them. A dollar a vote and the winners get theirs matched dollar for dollar by the furniture store."

"That doesn't seem fair to you. Your time is worth as much as anyone else's."

Holly shrugged. "It's good exposure and I asked to do it. I figure some of the groups would drop out at the last minute and I was right. Don't worry, I'll make the most of this."

Adam unearthed a small container of dip for the vegetables. "You always play all the angles, don't you?"

"I have to," Holly snapped, irritated. "You know, if I were a man, I'd be admired for being a real go-getter. But that's not considered an attribute in a woman."

"I didn't mean it to be a criticism," Adam stated quietly. "Just a comment. You put quite a lot of pressure on yourself. It must get tiring."

"I can't afford to get tired." Holly stood and brushed the crumbs from her camel slacks. "You're good with treetops. See if you can get this angel up there. And please...don't tangle the ribbons."

"I haven't eaten my sandwich, yet," Adam protested.

"You can eat later."

"Slave driver," he complained as he rewrapped his sandwich.

Holly whirled around, her brown eyes intense. "This is exactly what I was afraid of. I didn't ask you to come. In fact, I specifically told you not to. I'm *working,* Adam. Working. This is what I do for a living. How well I live depends on how hard I work."

She took a deep breath, conscious that her voice was louder than it needed to be. "And I've got my sisters to consider, too. Everything depends on me. My business is seasonal. I'm trying to expand, but for now, I've got three income-producing months out of the year. That means one of my working days is worth four of yours. If you can't accept that, I understand. But if you want to see me, it will have to be on my terms. It's selfish and I know it. But that's the way it has to be."

The emotional torrent of words ran out about the same time as her breath. She faced him, breathing quickly and waited for him to tell her off, pack up all that lovely food and stalk out of the showroom.

"Want a hug?" he asked softly, already reaching for her.

Holly's face crumpled as his arms closed around her and held her tightly.

"Been rough, has it?" One of his hands gently caressed her curls as she rested her head against his shoulder.

"Yes."

"Tell me about it some time?" His voice was gentle.

"Yes."

"Holly?"

Holly shuddered and lifted her head.

Adam's hold relaxed. His fingers tilted her chin until she was forced to look at him. "Have I complained about your work?"

"No," she answered honestly.

"I won't. You've come into my life at a time when I have emotional energy to spare. To give. It won't always be that way." He noted the wariness in her eyes and let her study him. "I don't think you know how to be a taker."

He surprised her. "What does that mean?"

"Just what it sounds like. The world is full of givers and takers. You've been a giver for so long, you can't take without feeling guilty."

Holly disentangled her arms from his and ran a shaky hand through her hair. "You sound like a pop psychologist." She couldn't believe he was still there. Anyone else would have left long ago. *She* would have left long ago. Well, she'd warned him. He knew exactly what he would be getting into. Okay. Fine.

"Thanks for being so understanding." Holly took a deep breath and smiled. "Now, would you hang that angel?"

"No."

Her smile disappeared and her jaw wore a militant look.

One of his dimples appeared. "I'm going," he said with quiet finality, "to eat my sandwich. Now."

CHAPTER FOUR

"WHY CAN'T YOU USE a bank like everyone else?" Laurel followed Holly into the large walk-in pantry and watched as her sister sorted foil-wrapped packets.

"I do. Where do you think I get money? Open the freezer for me, will you?"

Laurel yanked up the heavy white door. "I was getting lunch out, anyway. Holly," she began as Holly placed the packets into neatly, but misleadingly, labeled plastic bins. "Don't you think the money would be safer in a bank?"

Holly smiled grimly. "I happen to like cold hard cash."

"Give me a break."

"Shh. I'm counting and my fingers are freezing."

"Well, hurry up. I'm hungry."

Holly looked pointedly at Laurel's statuesque curves. "You're always hungry. Thought about going on a diet?"

"Cheap and miserly, that's what you are."

"Yeah, but that's twelve tax packets. We've got a roof over our heads until next December, but we can't eat after April. Although—" Holly studied her sister consideringly "—we could feast well into May if one of us would try to lose a few pounds."

"I lost five pounds in October!"

"We *all* lost five pounds in October." Holly moved aside as Laurel reached into the freezer. "What's for lunch?"

Laurel gave her a smug smile. "Alumnae Coffee leftovers again. This will be our third free meal, so no more comments on my appetite."

Holly nodded. "Point taken."

Laurel dug around in the freezer. "What's that?" she gestured to a frosty container.

"Ivy's college money. If all goes well, she can enroll for the spring semester."

"Finally." Laurel pulled out a bag of frozen sandwiches and meat tarts. "We've got to finish the raw veggies today. They're looking grim."

"Make soup."

"Out of what?"

"Don't we have a can of tuna or something?" Holly glanced at the bare shelves around them.

"Yuck. I'll send Ivy to the store." Laurel slammed the freezer door shut. "Seriously, Holly, I feel nervous having that much cash around."

Holly gave her a wry smile. "It isn't that much. Besides, I'd rather have my assets frozen here than in the bank."

"It wouldn't happen again," Laurel said quietly.

Holly turned out the light in the pantry and headed back into the kitchen. "It *won't* happen again. Anyway," she said after spending a few minutes at her ledger, "it cuts out impulse spending. Why do you think I made the American Express card into an ice cube?"

Laurel muttered something about microwaves as Ivy burst into the kitchen carrying their fur jacket on one arm and the black skirt, which one of the sisters usually wore daily, on the other.

"I just wanted to let you know I took these out of your closet, Laurel. I'm going to wear them tomorrow."

"Sorry. I'm going out to lunch after church."

"I've been invited to the Cowboy game. On one of my *rare* outings," Ivy said with a significant look at Holly. "I ran into a bunch of my friends. They're home for Christmas break. They've got extra tickets, so it won't cost anything."

Holly's sigh went unheard by either sister. "Maybe you can both wear the outfit. What time is kickoff?"

"Two. Tony's picking me up at noon."

"Noon!" Laurel glared at Holly. "What are you suggesting, that Ivy just strip me on the church steps?"

"Please, Laurel?" Ivy looked pleadingly from sister to sister. "Wear the red silk. Holly probably doesn't need it."

"Wear Holly's camel outfit," Laurel countered. "It still looks chic."

"It looks chic on Holly. It looks dumb on me. The pants are too long and I don't have the right shoes. At least with the skirt, I can wear my boots. I need the jacket to keep warm." Ivy hugged the furry softness to her cheek.

"Huh-uh."

"Come on! It's supposed to be *our* jacket." Ivy held it out of Laurel's reach. "How come I never get to wear it?"

"But to a football game?" Laurel looked to Holly for support. "She'll probably spill mustard on it."

"Laurel!" Holly ran her fingers through her curls. "It's okay, Ivy. Why don't you go put everything on and we'll help you pick your jewelry."

Ivy beamed. "Thanks, Holly!"

"She'll look like a little kid playing dress-up." Laurel shoved the cookie sheet with the leftovers into the oven.

"Laurel, she wants to wear the jacket to impress her friends. You know how they all but dropped her when they went off to college. And *they'll* be dressed to the teeth."

"That jacket was never meant to be hers," Laurel said resentfully.

"There wasn't any name on the package." Holly said quietly. "We'll never know which of us Mom and Dad intended to have it."

A howling from deep in the house made Holly roll her eyes. "What now?" she asked herself as it grew louder.

"It's not fair! Look what she did!" Ivy began crying with deep anguished sobs as she thumped down the stairs.

Holly ran to the bottom of the steps. "What's wrong?"

"Look!" Ivy pulled at the folds of sweater hanging on her slender frame. "She . . . she stretched all the sweaters!"

Holly sighed. "That one probably needs to be cleaned, anyway. We'll have the cleaners block it back into shape," she said soothingly.

"But what'll I wear?" Ivy wailed.

"You know that new red turtleneck we got on sale? You can be the first one to wear it."

"Really? Gosh, thanks, Holly!" Ivy smiled through her tears and whirled back up the stairs.

Holly felt a gut-wrenching twist of guilt, regret and a flare of the old anger, which melted into pity. Little Ivy had been hit hardest. Teenagers could be so cruel.

Holly sat on the bottom step, head on her knees. "Little" Ivy was nineteen. Nineteen and thrilled to be the first to wear a sweater they would all share. How pathetic.

She sat that way until she heard Gus's distinctive tapping on the front door.

"Are those the proofs?" Holly asked when she noticed the brown envelope Gus held.

"Hello to you, too, pretty lady." He sniffed. "What do I smell?"

"Lunch," answered Holly, resignedly gesturing him in.

"What? That time already?" Gus exclaimed in mock surprise.

"As you well know, moocher."

Gus eyed her expectantly. "Didn't Beth Robinson call you?"

"No, why?" Holly gripped his arm. "Gus, is it the cover?"

"Sure 'nough. Take a look at these." He handed her the envelope.

Holly fumbled with the clasp a fraction of a second before ripping open the flap and drawing out the photographs. "Gus, they're gorgeous!"

Gus pointed to the photograph on the top of the stack. "This one is Beth's choice for the cover. Said she was going to call you for some more information about Deck the Halls."

"You sweetie!" Holly restrained her impulse to plant a kiss on his fuzzy cheek and settled for a careful hug.

"Look here." Gus took the pictures from her and shuffled through them. "I sold this to your boyfriend's law firm. Can you believe they were going to go the smoked-turkey route for Christmas? When they saw this, they ordered copies for a bunch of their clients."

"They didn't mention the change in design?"

"Huh?"

"Never mind. There's the bearskin rug." Holly pointed. "You got the fireplace tools with the logo. Nice touch."

"Profitable touch. You ought to get some business from this, too."

Holly felt a weight lift from her shoulders. "Gus, dear friend, are you free for lunch? Laurel should have it ready about now."

Gus grinned, his teeth showing bright against the unshaven face. "I can work it in."

Holly entered the kitchen, more lighthearted than she remembered being in ages. "We're setting another place, Laurel. A soon-to-be-famous photographer is dining with us."

"Such an occasion will necessitate a trip to the freezer." Laurel raised her eyebrows in a silent question, which Holly answered with a quick affirming nod. "And what's the occasion?"

Holly swept her ledgers off the table. "The cover of *Town Square* magazine! Take a look at these." She handed the packet to Laurel and went to get the silverware.

Gus grabbed her elbow. "Holly? You think I could use that set for some more pictures?"

Holly shrugged. "You'll have to ask Adam." She tried to tug her arm away.

"Hol-ly." Gus sighed impatiently. "I don't want to give him a chance to say no. I . . . already signed a contract."

"Gus!" She regained possession of her elbow.

"Oh, come on. You know you can't get ahead by following rules." He gave her a disgusted look. "Just let me know when the Yankee's going to be gone and I'll pop in then."

"I *don't* have the key," Holly pointed out.

"Get it." Gus threw out his arms. "You're palling around with him. Or haven't things progressed that far?"

"Holly, weren't you thinking of asking Adam over for a thank-you dinner?" Laurel inserted smoothly.

Holly deliberately took a deep breath. "Yes, some-time—"

"You and Adam would have more privacy at the pent-house and Gus could take his photographs while you're cooking."

"We won't need—"

"You could get the key from Adam and have a nice dinner waiting for him. It would leave you plenty of time to chitchat about his . . . briefs, or whatever else was on his mind." Laurel composedly turned back to the stove.

Holly ignored Gus's snicker. She did owe him a favor. He'd suggested her company when *Town Square* first approached the law firm. His photographs were first-rate and he'd always been willing to finish out a roll of film and let her have the photos to show prospective clients. Now, thanks to him, one of her designs would be on the cover of the popular city magazine.

"So-o-o—" she endured the brotherly arm he put around her "—all I want is a little time in an empty apartment. Nothing illegal—I'll come in the front door and march right by the rent-a-cop downstairs."

"Gus," she sighed, "I don't want to bother Adam with this."

"He doesn't need to know. You give people too much information and it clutters their mind."

"Gus, it isn't that I don't appreciate what you've done—"

"I'd be crazy not to stay on the right side of three gorgeous babes." Gus released her.

Holly laughed. "You just want to make sure you have some place to stay when things are a little tight."

"Hey, I pay for it in pictures. You think film is free?"

"Speaking of which, have you got a couple of extras here? That was a new design."

His teeth gleamed in a sarcastic smile. "That's my girl. Always hustling."

"I've got to, Gus." Holly flipped through the pictures, selecting the ones for her portfolio.

"They're still in the kitchen, I think," Ivy's voice called from the hallway. "Hey, look who I found at the front door."

Holly looked up as Adam followed her youngest sister into the kitchen. His eyes sought hers immediately and the dimpled grin flashed. Dinner alone with Adam? In the penthouse with the glorious view? Well, she owed him, too, didn't she?

"I rang the bell and knocked," he explained.

"That's okay." Ivy went to investigate the lunch possibilities. "The doorbell doesn't ring in this part of the house anymore. Next time, come around to the back."

"Adam, we were just discussing you," Laurel announced in her best sultry movie-queen voice, ignoring

Holly's outraged warning glare. "And your marvelous penthouse."

Adam's smile included all of them, but lingered on Holly. "Just temporarily mine, I'm afraid."

"Have a seat." Gus shoved a chair toward him. "And take a look at these." He snatched the pictures from Holly.

"We were just having lunch," she said loudly. "Would you care to join us?"

"I had no intention of inviting myself," Adam protested, but not too strongly.

"That's okay, we're used to it." Ivy set a bowl of fruit on the table and tore off a couple of grapes for herself.

"Anyway, this guy I know went really wild over the shots," Gus was saying, and Holly cringed.

"We're having a light lunch, Adam, but Holly will make it up to you, won't you Holly?" Laurel gave her a sisterly hug and scooted out of the range of Holly's elbow.

"Naturally, I planned—"

"I'd like another crack at it before Holly takes the tree down." Gus used his earnest voice. "You know...to make some pocket money."

The best she could hope for, Holly decided, was that Adam wouldn't think what was turning out to be the world's most blatant setup was her idea.

Laurel slipped into Holly's usual place at the round table, leaving the chair next to Adam vacant. An oblivious Ivy quietly devoured the grapes.

"Fine with me," Adam answered as Holly sat down beside him. "What day?"

"I'm flexible," Gus shrugged. "Anytime."

"How about when Holly fixes you dinner, Adam?" Laurel bypassed Gus and pushed the sandwich plate toward Adam.

"I haven't had a chance to discuss it with him." As Holly spoke, Adam caressed her wrist and laced his fingers through hers. Holly felt an instant jolt that shot up her arm and lodged deep in her stomach. "Yet." She turned widened eyes to the man beside her. His brilliant blue eyes regarded her steadily.

"She'd planned to have it at your penthouse," Laurel prompted, since Holly had apparently lost all power of speech.

Adam gently squeezed her hand. "What about Wednesday?"

Holly squeezed back. "Wonderful."

IF SHE HADN'T BEEN dreaming about blue eyes and a funny feeling in the pit of her stomach, she wouldn't be in this mess, Holly thought, as the Wednesday-morning job ran late. And she was having trouble making the simplest decisions, like what to have for The Dinner. Laurel and Ivy had cheerfully donated Monday and Tuesday's meal money, which made Holly suspicious. Not of Ivy, who was a sweetie, but of the ever-ravenous Laurel, who was not.

Holly quickly walked into the lobby of the building where her next job was scheduled and headed for the telephones.

"Laurel, I'm running late. Can you go to the store for me?"

"Sure."

"You're being awfully nice. Why?"

"The more time you spend with Adam, the less work I have to do. What are you cooking?"

"I don't know," Holly said irritably. "How about Rock Cornish hens? Get a couple, plus some wild rice—"

"Feed the man some meat, Holly. Does he look like a wimp to you?"

A vision of Adam instantly flashed into her mind. She sighed.

"Right," Laurel said in her syrupy drawl. "You don't feed prissy food to a man like Adam. I figured you'd run late, so I already got a couple of steaks and some potatoes.''

''That's not very impressive,'' Holly protested.

''But easy.'' Laurel's sultry laugh sounded in Holly's ear. ''You don't plan to spend all your time cooking, do you?''

Holly swallowed, her mouth dry. This dinner was going to get her into trouble. On the other hand, how threatening could steak and potatoes be?

Two and a half hours later, Holly rode the plush elevator up to the penthouse, pleased at having made up some lost time.

At least she was pleased until the doors whispered open.

''Hey, babe!'' Gus's jaunty smile was strained around the edges.

''What is this?'' Holly stared in disbelief at the remnants of the once-elegant room, too stunned to realize immediately what was going on.

Gus turned his back to her and brazened it out. ''Don't worry, you won't bother me.'' He waved negligently. ''I won't need the kitchen.''

Holly climbed over the back of an armchair, which was jammed into the foyer, along with most of the living-room furniture.

Gus, visibly nervous, watched her progress. ''Look out for the cords.''

''Relax, Gus. They're too heavy to use for strangling you.'' Holly's foot caught on a tripod supporting an umbrella reflector. It teetered and Gus leapt to steady it. Then Holly saw the rest of the room. Mounds of feathers and filmy lingerie were heaped on the white silk sofa. Holly peered into a cardboard box. ''What is this stuff?'' She grabbed a handful of minuscule scraps of fabric and some leather…things, momentarily diverted. ''How do you wear this?'' she wondered aloud.

''Which one?''

Holly's head jerked up and she dropped her handful. "Bianca!"

"Who?" Gus croaked nervously, prudently remaining out of reach.

"My bear. She's wearing glasses and has an apple in her mouth." Holly glared at Gus accusingly.

He shrugged. "Back to school."

Holly repeated the words silently. She bent down and picked up an Easter basket, a couple of American flags and a stray shamrock. "You . . . you took all the snowflakes off my tree!"

"Just borrowed 'em." Gus gestured toward Holly's tree. "I've been putting 'em back."

Holly followed the trail. She found a bow and arrow with a heart at its tip. "Too bad August doesn't have a major holiday, Gus." She rescued a pilgrim hat from the corner.

"Oooh! These feathers tickle!" A bright giggle preceded the entrance of a flaming redhead. "Hi, honey," she warbled as she passed Holly. "Oh, good. You found the hat. Just put it on the bear, will ya? Oops!" She giggled again and grabbed a slipping turkey-feather boa. "Gus, I don't know if these pins will hold."

"Get out!" Holly's eyes blazed furiously. "Now!" She threw her armload in the general direction of the cardboard box.

"M-my stuff." Sweat beaded on Gus's forehead.

"Here!" Holly picked up the entire box and heaved it toward him. Gus lunged for it and the umbrella reflector crashed to the floor.

"I should have known you were up to something scummy!" Holly snatched up a handful of white netting from the sofa. The tiara attached to it provided a nice weight and the whole thing arced like a comet as it went zinging through the air.

"Hey—that's rented!"

Holly vented her fury by throwing the rest of the lingerie. The flimsy fabric couldn't hurt anything. She wasn't so angry she didn't consider that.

"Holly—babe—I've never seen you like this." Gus swatted at the sheer materials.

"And you, too, turkey." Holly threw a handful the redhead's way.

"Now wait a minute, honey. We haven't done November yet and I went to a lot of trouble to fix this cute feather bikini."

"Holly! Have you gone completely insane?" Laurel shouted from the elevator.

"You!" Holly gulped air and glared at her sister.

Laurel tossed her mane of streaked hair. "Come into the kitchen and we'll discuss this."

"There's nothing to discuss." Holly took one more deep breath and then bent to gather some of the littered props. "Do you realize that Adam could be here any minute?"

"Nonsense," Laurel said, briskly carrying a grocery sack into the kitchen. "It's only four-thirty."

Holly hesitated, glaring at Gus. "Get out." Her voice trembled with anger. "You, too." She pointed at Miss November and followed Laurel. "Did it occur to you that Adam might take off early to be with me?"

"No," Laurel said, unconcerned. "If Adam takes off early, it will be to buy you flowers, or a bottle of the perfect wine. That man knows how to make the most of an opportunity and he's been holding back too long."

Holly blinked. "You knew about this, didn't you?"

"As much as you did." Laurel began unloading the sack.

"I did *not* know Gus was taking sleazy pictures of some turkey." The corner of Holly's eye caught a flash. "I suppose he's doing November now."

"He might as well finish."

"Adam's been really great to us. He trusted us. Me. And how does he get repaid?"

"A fabulous steak dinner. That is, if you ever cook it."

"Gus shouldn't have been here alone," Holly protested.

"He wasn't. The redhead works as a receptionist for Adam's firm. Gus met her when he sold them the other pictures."

Holly moaned.

"You are just determined to be unpleasant about this whole thing, aren't you?" Laurel slammed a jar of cinnamon on the counter. "After shopping for *your* groceries, I got here and checked the cabinets to see if you needed spices or anything. You didn't have any flour."

"So?"

"You can't make an apple pie without it."

"Is that dessert?"

Laurel smiled slyly. "If you've got time. I got a couple of pastries as backups in case you get distracted and the pie burns. I thought they could double as breakfast, if dinner drags on later than you planned."

"This is *not* a seduction," Holly said firmly.

"It should be," Laurel retorted as she drifted out of the kitchen.

Holly sank onto the stool by the telephone and stared into the narrow kitchen. How could she tell Adam any of this? She ran both hands through her curls. It made them all look like opportunistic users. And maybe Gus was like that, but she and Laurel weren't, not deep down.

Adam had been so... Sweet was the word that popped into her mind, but that didn't describe Adam. He'd been tolerant of them, so far. Holly knew it was because he was attracted to her.

She slowly emptied the plastic sack of Granny Smith apples and began to peel them. Adam had allowed her to set the terms of their relationship. She winced, uncomfortable that everything so far had gone her way. Holly heard Gus and Laurel leave and went out to inspect the living area. It wasn't too bad. She spent a few minutes straightening and putting knickknacks back as she remembered. The tree was a mess, of course. Holly shrugged and returned to the kitchen to roll out pie dough.

Twenty minutes later, she grudgingly admitted that Laurel's instincts hadn't failed her. The penthouse kitchen was tiny and not intended for elaborate meal preparation. The pie made a big mess, but the rest of the meal would be simple to prepare. Holly's breath caught at the price of the steaks. Did Laurel have to be so extravagant?

Wasn't Adam worth it? countered an inner voice as she slapped the meat on the fancy countertop grill. The potatoes baked with the pie and Laurel had included a slice of pâté, crackers, but no wine.

Holly had just carried the pâté out to the living area when she heard the elevator. Adam was later than she'd expected and she was glad she'd had the extra time to compose herself. She stood in the foyer, feeling slightly awkward.

Adam's face lit up when he saw her. He *was* worth it. Surprising herself, Holly reached for him. "Hello." Her voice was low and husky.

It barely registered that his arms were full of elongated brown sacks and a bouquet of flowers. He quickly set them on the floor in time to wrap his arms around her.

Holly wasn't sure what she'd originally intended, but it hadn't included fusing herself to him. She wasn't ready for the incredible melting sensation, or the excitement that seemed to sparkle through her whole body. Amazed at her response, Holly shakily attempted to disengage herself.

"Don't stop now." Adam lightly brushed her lips with his.

"I think I'd better." She laid a trembling hand on his shoulder.

"Not yet." He spoke quietly, all the while inching his lips closer and closer to hers.

Holly's first thought was to resist; then she remembered the explosive sparkles of a moment before.

An instant later, Adam's lips touched hers. He gradually, but deliberately, increased the pressure, unhurriedly moving his lips against hers until he felt the last of her resistance melt.

Holly felt it, too. Her will drained out of her, leaving her insides shaking so much, she knew Adam had to be aware of it.

They broke the kiss simultaneously, each breathing in quick shallow breaths.

"I—" Holly stammered, not having any idea what to say next. "I had no idea you could kiss like that!" she blurted.

Adam threw her a sexy half smile. "I know."

In a daze, Holly found that, yes, her legs still worked, and led Adam toward the pâté.

She sank, wordlessly, onto the white sofa. Adam retrieved the paper bags and the flowers. "These are for you."

"Thank you." Her voice was a husky whisper.

Adam smiled perceptively. "I'll put them in water."

"That's my line." She managed a short laugh.

Working at Exemplary Temporaries wasn't so bad, she began to rationalize as Adam walked toward the kitchen. And maybe the business boom they'd been expecting wouldn't materialize anyway.

What was she thinking? She gave herself a mental shake. She wasn't about to let a few kisses jeopardize Deck the Halls. In spite of her recent actions, Adam had better realize that.

"I saw the steaks and smelled the pie. Dinner's going to be great." Adam poured her a glass of wine, then sat beside her, casually stretching his arm along the back of the sofa.

This was going to be harder than she'd thought. Adam's hand on her shoulder gently urged her to relax against him. She did, enjoying the warmth of his body next to hers. The fire Gus had built flickered gently, reducing itself to a bed of glowing embers.

"I...didn't mean to get quite so carried away earlier." She spoke slowly and quietly, easing her words into the companionable silence.

Adam rested his head against hers and she could hear the steady beating of his heart. "There's no going back, Holly."

Holly felt a choking lump in her throat. She nodded, unable to speak.

"I'm willing to be patient—not forgotten."

Holly smiled sadly. Adam might think he could be patient, but she knew better. He'd interfere, resent her work and become more and more demanding. Then they'd have a big fight and that would be the end of it.

The timer on the stove went off. "I'll bet that's the pie." Adam planted a kiss on her forehead. "I'll go change while you take it out of the oven."

Holly sat up, then turned and gave Adam a fierce hug. *Please wait for me,* she pleaded silently, because if he wouldn't and she had to choose, Holly wasn't so certain that Deck the Halls would win.

The aroma of warm apple pie surrounded her as she tore lettuce for their salad. She concentrated fiercely on her task and avoided thinking about the man changing his clothes. She succeeded so well that she didn't hear Adam's approach. She had only a momentary warning as gentle fingers pushed aside the curls at the nape of her neck and soft lips kissed it.

Holly reacted immediately. Her stomach contracted, pulsing with each of the butterflylike kisses Adam placed on her neck.

"Adam." She sighed his name.

Hands on her shoulders, Adam slowly turned her to face him.

What had happened in the minutes since he left her? She thought they understood one another, that they'd agreed their relationship would have to wait until . . . until what?

"Adam," Holly whispered again. He wore the blue cashmere sweater and she couldn't resist sliding her fingers over the inviting softness covering his chest, up to the firm muscles of his shoulders and neck.

Their lips met as Holly's fingers entangled themselves in the blue-black hair curling behind Adam's neck.

All her ideas about controlling their relationship were swept away. She pressed closer to Adam and found herself held in a bone-crushing embrace.

It was Adam who parted her lips and Adam's tongue that met hers in a slow leisurely dance. It was Adam, in fact, who was very much in control and Holly who was fast losing it.

At the precise moment when Holly felt she would faint if the two of them didn't throw themselves onto the kitchen floor, he set her from him.

Smiling tenderly, he gently caressed her cheek, then reached around her and shut off the grill where the sizzling steaks hissed and popped. Only then did Holly notice the slightly charred smell.

Adam placed his hand on the small of her back and gently urged her through the door. Holly took a step and stumbled.

"My knees," she said with an apologetic laugh.

"Ah, my cue," Adam slipped an arm under her shoulders and lifted her against his chest. "I've always wanted to do this," he said as he carried her into the bedroom. He stopped by the edge of the bed and looked down at her.

"Now what?" Holly whispered.

A muscle worked in Adam's jaw. "In a move of exquisite finesse, I shall set you gently on the bed. Isn't that how it's supposed to go?"

Uncertainty warred with passion. Holly's teeth tugged at her lower lip. "Maybe not."

"Okay." Adam tossed her unceremoniously onto the center of the bed.

Caught off guard, Holly bounced a couple of times as Adam crawled toward her.

"Why did you do that?" Her face was a portrait of confused sensuality.

Adam propped himself on one elbow. "I don't want to be predictable."

Holly pushed Adam squarely in the center of his chest and pinned his arms to the bed. "Neither do I."

She felt his muscles tense slightly just before he freed himself and pinned her in an identical position. "Yield?" Without waiting for an answer, Adam covered her mouth with his.

It had been so long since a man had held her in his arms and kissed her. Had it ever felt like this? If so, how had she been able to numb her feelings?

"Holly?" Adam nuzzled the side of her neck.

"Hmm?"

Adam raised his head so he could study her face. "What changed your mind?"

"About what?" Puzzled, Holly shook her head. Adam smiled and reached toward the floor beside the bed, bringing up a handful of red chiffon.

Holly blanched.

"I got the message." Adam held the nightie up by the straps. It was completely transparent, except for three strategically placed patches of black lace.

It was hideous.

And it meant she'd have to tell Adam about Gus's latest project. Furthermore, she was not flattered to realize Adam thought she ordered her sleepwear from trashy catalogs.

"Quite a departure from your usual look."

"Yes, uh, no. It's...not mine." She didn't want to explain. She felt guilty and embarrassed by the whole episode.

"You borrowed it?"

"Kiss me, Adam."

Holly put everything she had into that kiss, determined to turn Adam's brain into putty, or at the very least, make him forget about the garish nightie he'd discovered.

He held back, not responding the way she'd hoped. His insides should be jelly by now.

She'd show him. She reached under the softness of the cashmere and splayed her hands across his chest, feeling a tremor. Holly was so caught up in her determined seduction of Adam, she failed to realize that she was the one who was trembling. Her brain was putty; her insides were jelly.

Adam felt the tremor, too. Enjoyable as the last few minutes had been, he wasn't fooled. Holly was trying to convince herself that she was still entangled in a web of passion. But she wasn't now. That vulgar scrap of material had changed everything, and Holly was obviously trying to overcome second thoughts.

He couldn't go through with it. Holly was much too special for him to indulge in a lusty fling. No, he was going to be noble. He'd wait just long enough to give her something to think about—and then he'd do the right thing. If he could.

Holly eased the sweater off Adam's shoulders and over his head in a quick movement that caught him by surprise.

Adam's heart thundered in his ears. Any minute now he'd be noble and stop this. He exhaled sharply as Holly moved against him, fitting herself against his length. Any minute now, he told himself as his arms pressed into her back, pulling her even closer. Any minute.

Holly raised her lips to his once more and then, incredibly, Adam's hands were on her shoulders, pushing her away.

He breathed heavily, his eyes closed, as she watched in dazed puzzlement. With a sigh, he rested his forehead on hers.

"Enough."

"It doesn't have to be," Holly whispered.

Adam dropped a light kiss on her forehead and rolled to a sitting position on the bed. He drew one more deep breath, opened his eyes and smiled crookedly at her.

Holly lay on the bed, her lips full and parted, her hair charmingly mussed.

Adam reached for the discarded red nightie. Holly immediately bolted to a sitting position. "Adam," she began determinedly, "I'd like to explain."

He shook his head. "No. You're entitled to change your mind. No reason necessary."

"*I* didn't!"

"Yes, you did, and it's okay." Adam paused for a moment, staring at the black-and-red chiffon. A brief flicker of his imagination had Holly wearing it. "Holly," he began slowly.

"It's this stupid thing." Holly snatched it from him, wadded it up and flung it into the wastebasket. "It was a mistake."

"It isn't stupid," Adam disagreed. "And it doesn't bother me that you've changed your mind," he said again. He ignored the frustrated ache in his belly. "Though I'll admit this isn't your style."

"I should be apologizing to you." Holly hesitated uncertain how to begin the embarrassing explanations.

"Don't." Adam placed a finger over her lips. "We don't have to rush into a physical relationship. I told you casual affairs have never appealed to me. I want to get to know you better. Then sex becomes a communication of the soul, as well as the body.''

I don't deserve him, Holly thought as guilt tore through her again. ''That's beautiful.'' She reached out to draw her fingers along his cheek.

Adam caught her hand, turned her palm and placed a kiss in the center of it. ''I don't want to rush you. And I'm not prepared for this just now, in any way. I'm all for spontaneity—not recklessness.'' One of his dimples appeared. ''Of course later we could renegotiate.''

CHAPTER FIVE

"THIS HAS GOT TO BE the classiest warehouse around." Laurel stood, hands on well-rounded hips, surveying the living room.

"Can't beat the rent." Holly smiled briefly and went back to her notebook. In the distance, the telephone rang.

"I'll get it," shouted Ivy.

"You don't suppose that's another job, do you?" Laurel stopped at the bottom of the stairs.

"I hope so."

"You would. I don't understand all these people who wait until the last minute."

"Isn't it great?" Holly's face creased in a smile. "Anyway, two weeks before Christmas is not the last minute. December twenty-fourth at one o'clock in the afternoon is."

"That's still a possibility."

"Another Chili Christmas!" Ivy yelled from the study.

Holly groaned. "That's the last one."

"Holly, that one and Merry Texmas are our most popular trees this year." Laurel started up the stairs. "Bloomie said she could get as many crystals as we needed."

"They're costing us a fortune. We have to rent each tree twice before we break even. What if nobody wants it next year?"

"Quit worrying. Next year, you take off the chili-pepper lights, leave the crystals and call it New Age Christmas or Crystal Christmas. Merry Texmas isn't about to go out of style and you can use the chili-pepper lights on that."

"But we still won't make a profit until the year after that."

"Okay, don't take off the chili-pepper lights and call it Fire and Ice."

Holly scribbled in her notebook. "That's great, Laurel."

"Some of us think about things other than money."

Ivy came into the room in time to hear that last exchange. "Is she still going on about profit margins?"

Laurel nodded.

"Holly, just think about the four sorority- and one fraternity-house trees we're dismantling tomorrow and the fact that so far you've rented two of those for a second time this season. Twice the profit. That's a first."

Holly flipped to the scheduling calendar. "I can't believe it's already the middle of December."

"I can!" Laurel and Ivy said at the same time. They chattered amiably as they climbed upstairs to the bedrooms where the decorations were stored.

Holly scheduled another Chili Christmas, wincing at the cost and number of ornaments.

"Time for a dinner break?" Laurel asked hopefully as she and Ivy lugged another box downstairs. "I wonder what Adam will bring tonight."

"It isn't right to expect him to bring us food all the time," Holly protested.

"But he does," Ivy said.

On cue, the doorbell rang. "Ah, dinner!" Laurel said softly, an arched eyebrow directed toward Holly.

Holly gave her a warning glance.

"I'll go get some napkins and drinks." Ivy dropped her box and hurried into the kitchen.

Holly made an exasperated sound as Laurel flung open the front door.

"Why, Adam, what a nice surprise! Holly, honey," Laurel drawled, "It's Adam. Isn't that nice?"

Holly opened her mouth to protest.

Adam walked in, carrying flat cardboard boxes, exuding the mouth-watering aroma of pepperoni and Italian spices. "Hey, busy night! Congratulations. Let me save you some time, here, Holly." He headed toward the kitchen.

"Bring your sister," he instructed Laurel. "Where were we? I know—you tell me I shouldn't have. I say it's no trouble, just a couple of pizzas. Then I say I like to spoil you, and no, I won't take your money. Okay, next time it's your treat, et cetera, et cetera."

Silence.

"Laurel and Ivy want pizza, don't you?" Adam asked with an amused look at them.

"Please, Holly, please, please? Pretty please with pepperoni on top?" Laurel and Ivy pleaded, with outstretched hands.

Holly bit the insides of her cheeks. She would not encourage them.

Adam picked up one of the boxes and waved the aroma toward her. Nothing.

"Relax, Holly," he said as the others helped themselves. "I used coupons."

"I knew you were incorrigible," she said at last, taking the gooiest piece of pizza she could find.

"And you love it." Adam grinned.

"Yeah." Holly grinned back.

"So how goes the season? Are you ahead or behind projected income?"

"Ahead," Laurel answered. "You were an unexpected help with the food budget."

"Laurel!" Even though they all realized it was true, Holly hated to hear it admitted aloud.

"How many jobs do we have to pack for tomorrow?" Adam began clearing away the remains of their pizza dinner.

"Seven," Ivy replied.

"Hey, they're really beginning to pick up, aren't they?"

"And we take down five trees tomorrow. The semester has ended and all decorations have to be cleared before the dorms and houses close for winter break." Laurel followed the last two pieces of pizza over to the kitchen sink. Holly watched as she edged toward Adam while he sealed the leftovers in plastic wrap. Laurel grabbed at the pieces and Adam whisked them out of reach.

"That's tomorrow's breakfast, Laurel. You'll hate yourself in the morning."

He already knew all their little foibles, Holly realized.

"More boxes need to be hauled downstairs?" Adam asked.

"Adam, you don't need to help," Holly said automatically. Another ritual.

"I know." He smiled.

"You're going to anyway, aren't you?"

"Yes."

This time, instead of waving him up the stairs or assigning him some task, Holly tilted her head to one side. "Why?"

Adam tugged on one of her curls, hiding the fact that his fingers briefly caressed her cheek. "Because I want to be near you," he said in a low voice only she could hear. "And because I keep hoping you'll get caught up on the work and we can have some time alone."

Adam watched the guilt flash through Holly's expressive brown eyes. "You asked."

"So I did. Make an appointment for March. It's a quiet month."

"I like my plan better." Adam turned and walked into the living room. Approaching one of the seven piles of boxes and ornament cartons, he picked up the inventory sheet and began checking off the items.

Holly watched pensively. He knew the whole routine. What would she do if he quit coming after work every day?

HOLLY'S ALARM SCREECHED and she reached out to silence it. Every muscle in her body screamed in protest. Seven trees up and five down had meant a lot of lifting and stretching and bending.... She was still exhausted. Her eyelids scratched her eyes, which squinted from the bright winter sunlight pouring through her window. She'd never had a hangover, but suspected this was close to how one felt.

Coffee! She smelled coffee!

There was a tap on her door. "Holly?"

She opened her mouth to answer and managed a hoarse squeak.

"Holly?" Adam's voice sounded raspy. "I heard your alarm. I brought you some coffee."

Holly groped around for the jeans and baggy sweater she'd been wearing last night, or rather, early this morning when she'd collapsed on her bed. She hobbled toward the door, voice creaking. "Minute, Adam."

He stood there holding two mugs of coffee, one black, the other heavily laced with milk. He thrust the milky one at her. "Drink."

"Thanks." She drank.

"You look like I feel," she said, and discovered that her voice worked again.

Adam rolled bloodshot eyes at her and drained his coffee mug. He wore the same clothes he'd worn all day Saturday, too.

"You go through this every year?"

"No." Holly shook her head and looked inquiringly at the bottom of her mug.

"There's more downstairs."

"Anybody else awake?"

"Nope." Adam appeared disinclined to fetch her more coffee, so Holly reluctantly began to make her way downstairs.

They reached the kitchen after a silent procession from the second floor. Holly refilled their coffee mugs and slumped at the kitchen table. Adam slid into the seat next to her. He needed a shave.

"Yesterday was incredible," Holly began.

"Incredible is one way to describe it, yes. Hideously overscheduled even for a masochist like you is another."

"You didn't have to stay."

"I couldn't abandon you and your sisters." Adam took another sip of coffee. "Besides, my car was back here, remember?"

"So much for chivalry."

"I made coffee this morning. All you managed to do was hit your snooze control three times and wake me up."

"I did? Three times?"

Adam held up three fingers.

"Sorry." Holly sneaked a glance at Adam's disgruntled face. "You make great coffee."

"You always say that." He gave a tired smile. "I would've started breakfast, but . . ." He waved at the refrigerator and pantry.

Holly shrugged. "No time to shop and we're not much on breakfast."

"Figures." He sent her a stern look. "You don't have any more days like yesterday scheduled, do you?"

"I didn't do that on purpose. I didn't realize that when the university said all trees had to be down by the end of the term, they weren't going to make an exception for us."

"Why would they?"

"Because we're hired professionals. Since the students have to leave, it makes sense to have that rule for them. I assumed that since we're an outside business, we'd have more leeway."

"Now you know."

Holly grinned. "I know that seven up and five down in one day is about all we can handle."

"Next time, I *will* abandon you."

Holly wavered, then hesitantly touched Adam's arm before giving in to impulse and hugging him. It was the first physical intimacy she'd initiated since their dinner a few days earlier and she felt momentarily awkward.

Adam hauled her onto his lap. "Fair warning," he said, running his fingers along his beard. "You are about to be kissed."

His beard was rough and he tasted wonderfully of coffee.

"I see someone woke up and smelled the coffee," Laurel drawled as she padded across the kitchen floor to the pot. She pulled the ties of her silk kimono tighter and skimmed her fingers through expensively layered hair. It responded by framing her face in artful disarray. Pouring herself a cup of coffee, she leaned against the counter and silently regarded the two of them.

Holly tried to get up, but Adam held her fast. Rather than engage in an undignified struggle, she relaxed.

"Well." Laurel sipped her coffee and looked at them. "Did I see a blank day today, by chance?"

"Not by chance," Holly replied. "The *Town Square* magazine with our cover comes out tomorrow and I scheduled today as a buffer. All we have to do is check the light strings and load the van."

Adam's hand absently caressed her back. "Anticipating a flood of business?"

Holly looked down at him. "I hope so and I hope we get some party jobs out of it."

Laurel joined them at the table. "What's more likely to happen is that we'll get a whole batch of calls right near Christmas from frantic people who haven't left themselves enough time to do everything."

Adam didn't say any more. Holly knew he was disappointed that their work wasn't winding down. After yesterday's marathon, even she was beginning to get sick of it all.

"Got it." Laurel set her mug down. "We're having a lazy day today—no arguments from you, Holly. Adam, you're invited."

"For what?"

Laurel grinned. "There'll be food."

"Naturally," Holly murmured.

"We'll get a turkey—they're on sale this week, Holly—and have a big dinner with all the trimmings. You know, cranberry sauce and the whole bit."

"Sounds like work," Holly said, but she smiled.

"Not with the four of us." No one had noticed Ivy's appearance. "And we'll move the television in here and watch football all afternoon, right?" She went to the cabinets by the pantry and pulled down several cookbooks. "After lunch, we'll make Christmas cookies."

"We haven't done that in ages." Holly began to look forward to the rest of the day.

"Up," Adam ordered.

Holly climbed gingerly off his lap. "Leg numb?"

Adam's eyes twinkled as he pounded feeling back into his leg. "It was worth it."

"I'd better get to the store." Laurel rinsed her mug on the way out.

"Don't we have any juice? Hardly any milk... You caffeine addicts can't see beyond your morning fix," grumbled Ivy from the refrigerator. She grabbed a can of soda. "I can't believe I'm having Diet Coke for breakfast."

"Laurel will see to your nutritional needs for the rest of the day," Holly reassured her as another layer of guilt settled on her shoulders. When would she stop letting people down?

After a last look in the refrigerator, Ivy slammed the door. "I'll be in the pantry making a list. Think I'll go with Laurel to buy groceries."

"And I," Adam said, testing his leg, "will go home to shower and change."

Holly walked him to the door. "Hurry back. It won't be the same without you," she added, surprising herself.

Even worse, she thought, as she watched Adam's car follow the circular driveway to the street, nothing would ever be the same again. And she didn't *want* it to be the same again. "Watch it, Holly," she murmured to herself, "you're falling in love with him."

Her realization didn't spoil the afternoon, but it did make her intensely aware of Adam's every movement. When he approached, she felt the back of her neck prickle; her eyes darted to his constantly. More often than not, she found him watching her. He was never the first to break contact.

How could he be calm if he felt even half of what she did?

This was terrible. No wonder she'd avoided relationships for the past few years.

"Dishwasher is loaded and running," Laurel announced. "Ivy and I'll start the cookies."

Adam and Ivy were discussing what kind of cookies to make. Holly smiled benevolently as she finished the dishes left in the sink. Adam fit in with their family. Adam was kind to her sisters and a hard worker. Adam's touch melted her insides. She was obsessed with Adam.

What was the matter with her? How could she have allowed him through her defenses?

The back of her neck prickled. "I'll dry," Adam said softly standing right behind her.

They worked in companionable silence. "You've been really sneaky," Holly said at last.

"How so?"

She dipped a pot in the rinse water. "I've started to take you for granted. When I plan jobs, I assign you something to do and just assume you'll be there to do it. And you always are."

"Do you mind?" Adam tilted her chin until she met his eyes.

"I'm afraid," she told him.

"Of what?"

Holly dried her hands and wrapped her arms around Adam, unconcerned whether her sisters saw or not. It was frightening to realize how right it felt to be held by him. "I'm afraid of depending on you too much. Deck the Halls is almost there—we're just about to make it. And when we do, I want to say that we did it all on our own, without anyone's help."

"And you're worried I'll negate that achievement. You've got to do it all by yourself, or it doesn't count? Is that it?" For the first time since she'd met him, Adam's blue eyes were cold. Holly's arms slipped down.

He was exactly right, but he made it sound petty.

"Yes," Holly avowed. "And I have to prove I can make it on my own to everybody, especially the vultures who destroyed the business it took my dad a lifetime to build."

"And you lose points for accepting help?"

Holly's eyes flashed. "I don't want to be helpless anymore. I don't want to be helpless ever again." Her eyes burned, but she was an expert at fighting off tears.

"Hey!" Laurel exclaimed. "Now Adam, honey, Holly can be a—" Laurel hesitated, obviously bypassing the first word that came to mind "—slave driver, but you have no idea what she went through."

Holly's eyes widened at Laurel's unexpected defense.

"In the first place, she was just out of school with a brand-new shiny business degree and no job. She couldn't even look for one, because she ended up spending all her time with lawyers. I was still in college, Ivy was in high school and the bottom had fallen out of the price of oil. Even if Dad hadn't died, the company might have gone bust. Holly fought. Hard. But against those oilmen and their lawyers..." Laurel shook her head.

"They auctioned off everything. You know that Texas lets you keep your house, but you saw the rooms when you stayed last night." Laurel's expression dared him to comment.

"No furniture." Adam's voice was clipped.

"No food, either, for a while," Ivy added.

Adam threw her a startled glance, seeing her words confirmed in the faces of the other two.

Holly shrugged. "They froze the assets. I just didn't know how..." She splayed her hands expressively.

"But your lawyer should have seen to that!" Adam protested even as he remembered with sickening clarity Mr. Steele's refusal to help her. "You aren't supposed to starve!"

"We shopped for food in a certain department store's gourmet section, Adam. They very kindly issued us a brand-new credit card and never bothered to bill us." Holly's chin tilted.

"It was kind of fun, though, charging all that ritzy food. Now that we can pay for it, we can't afford it." Ivy laughed, and it broke the tension.

"I paid them back—every penny," Holly said.

"You would." Adam forced himself to smile. "I didn't know all the details of what happened. Now I understand why you so badly want to succeed—just don't overdo it, okay?"

Holly smiled back. "Okay."

"Well, now that you've finished your little spat," drawled Laurel, "let's make cookies."

"I miss making these for the hospital," Ivy said, a complete football game later.

"I think I've got a real artistic flair for sugar cookies." Adam gestured to his precisely decorated creations.

"It's peaceful sitting here doing this. You don't have to think." Holly looked around the kitchen, absorbing the warmth and inhaling the smell of vanilla.

"Cheap therapy." Laurel licked icing off her fingers. "Any more rejects?"

"Laurel!" Three voices protested in unison and dissolved into laughter.

"Holly, why can't we decorate the children's wing this year?" Ivy glanced at her sister as she reached for the icing.

Adam observed Holly's expression, choosing to remain silent. There was the guilt again. It was never far below the surface. Holly tried to do everything and if she achieved anything less than perfection, she felt she had failed.

"I left fliers at the hospital, Ivy." Laurel brought another rack of cookies to be decorated.

"No, I mean the way we did when Mom and Dad were alive."

"We can't afford to donate our time and supplies to the hospital anymore." Holly bit off each word, sounding harsher than Adam knew she intended. Her head was bent over the Christmas-tree cookie she was decorating, but Adam saw the stricken look. Here she was, decorating Christmas trees even during her time off.

Laurel looked from Ivy to Holly's bent head. "We could take over our leftovers on Christmas Eve, Holly. We won't get any more jobs after that."

Adam watched Holly compose her face. "We could," she said evenly, "but why would the hospital, or anyone in it, hire us if they knew we'd come by on Christmas Eve, any-way?"

"We wouldn't have to tell them," Ivy pleaded.

Holly dragged in a deep breath. "It took three years for them to stop expecting us to pick up as usual. We do it now, and we can write them off as a potential client."

"Money! That's all you ever think about!" Ivy ran from the kitchen.

Laurel scowled at her. "You never quit, do you?" She turned toward the door. "I'll go to Ivy."

There was an uncomfortable silence. "Aren't you going to leave, too?" Holly stared at Adam defiantly.

"No." Adam put his arm around her and pulled her to-ward him. "I'd waste a perfectly good opportunity." He kissed her, then drew back reluctantly. It wasn't what she needed now.

"You don't think I'm heartless?" She looked up at him, hurt visible in her brown eyes.

Adam cuddled her reassuringly, as he might a small child. "You've had to make some difficult and unpopular deci-sions." Holly laid her head on Adam's shoulder. He could smell the unusual scent she wore and satisfied himself with resting his cheek on the top of her head.

It was so rare to be alone with her, to be this close, that he found her nearness sweet torment. "Tell me why decorat-ing the hospital is so special."

"You know how my parents were about Christmas. Well, this was one of Mom's charities, and we started decorating the children's wing for Christmas each year. It got bigger and bigger. My . . . birthday is Christmas Eve . . ."

"Figures." Adam laughed softly. "How did your par-ents manage that?"

Holly raised her head. "They were always well orga-nized," she said, smiling. "Noelle is my middle name. They thought it was fate."

"This is too corny to be believed."

"It is not. I always felt special. Anyway, I never regretted having my birthday so close to Christmas. We'd be at the hospital and bring presents for the kids there. It was like a giant birthday party and I always felt happy I could go home and not have to stay at the hospital. Which is probably just what my parents were trying to teach me."

"I wish I could have met them," Adam said, regret vibrating in his voice.

Holly just nodded, unable to speak. "At any rate," she continued after a few moments, "it was the hospital decorations I used to start Deck the Halls, and Laurel and Ivy..." Her voice trailed off. Lifting her head, she scooted her chair away from Adam.

"You, sir, are addictive," she said in an attempt to lighten the mood.

"That's the whole idea." Adam handed her a cookie.

"Seriously, you've been a good friend. I didn't know how much I needed one until I met you." Even as she spoke, Holly knew he was more than that.

Adam's raised eyebrow, as he took a recently iced cookie for himself, told her he knew it, too.

CHAPTER SIX

"ADAM WOULD DO IT—I know he would!" Ivy held up a red velvet Santa costume as Holly shook her head doubtfully.

"Probably, but let's not ask him."

"Holly, honey," Laurel drawled, hands on hips, "you are going to have to decide how you feel about that man and go with it."

"Laurel, *honey*," Holly drawled back, glaring, "what does that have to do with asking him to wear Daddy's Santa suit while we decorate the hospital?"

"You're wearing Mama's Mrs. Claus outfit," Ivy stated as if that explained everything.

"Let's give him a break. Adam is around here all the time!"

Laurel raised her eyebrows. "Which ought to tell you something."

"Yes. We take advantage of him." Holly returned to her ever-present notebook.

"He doesn't mind—remember Sunday? If we don't ask him to come with us, he'll be hurt." Ivy shook out the costume, apparently hoping five years worth of wrinkles would magically fall away.

Holly relented. "Come with us, yes. Wear the Santa outfit, no."

Laurel poked through the hanging clothing bag. "I wonder if I can still get into my elf outfit?"

"Don't even try."

Laurel threw Holly a venomous glance. "I will overlook that remark. Holly, honey, your halfhearted protests aren't fooling anybody. Including Adam."

"Probably not, but I feel obligated to make them."

"That's the dumbest way to hook a man I ever heard of."

"I'm not trying to hook him!" Holly grabbed the phone. "I'm going to let him know when we're leaving."

"On the other hand, maybe it's pure genius. Maybe he likes the challenge."

"Oh, for heaven's sake, it's busy." Holly slammed down the phone. "I'm going over to his office," she announced, thinking it would be a good excuse to do so.

"Ask him about wearing the outfit?" Ivy grinned hopefully.

Holly bit her lip and tried to imagine Adam in the huge red suit. "Have the pillows ready." She got her coat. "And don't forget to pick up replacement bulbs for the two jobs we've got this afternoon."

It had been five years since Holly had been to the Swinehart, Cathardy and Steele offices. She'd asked for legal help. Not only did they plead conflict of interest—which she had heard countless times—they'd presented her with another in a mounting pile of bills.

She'd learned a lot that day. Old Mr. Steele had looked her right in the eye as he denied her request. Most of the other lawyers hadn't been able to do that, hiding behind a barrage of papers and legal terminology.

The typewriters were silent as Holly opened the glass doors and stepped into the muted gray of the outer office.

"Adam Markland?" she asked the flamboyant red-headed receptionist, whose eyes widened apprehensively.

"I'm Holly Hall," Holly introduced herself, adding dryly, "I don't believe we've met."

"Thanks." The woman sagged with relief and flicked a glance at the phone board. "He's on the telephone."

"He's still here, then."

"He never goes out for lunch." The woman answered one of the blinking lights on the switchboard.

The sound of Adam's voice as he spoke on the phone guided Holly to his office. She peered around the half-open door and slowly walked in.

Adam cradled the receiver between his ear and shoulder, scribbling furiously. Without looking up, he waved her in and stood up to feel for his wallet. He withdrew some money and shoved it toward her, never removing his eyes from his notes.

"Just a moment." Adam covered the mouthpiece. "Make it roast beef today, Darlene—" He looked up finally, and saw Holly, his face registering pleased astonishment.

In the few moments Holly stood by Adam's desk, she had a chance to see the stacks of file folders and bundles of papers covering every chair, sofa, filing cabinet and shelf in the office.

"Adam, you're busy so..." She waved and turned to leave.

Adam stretched across the desk and grabbed her arm, shaking his head. He held on, looking at her as he finished his phone conversation.

"Holly! What are you doing here?" Adam smiled delightedly as, still holding on to her arm, he walked around his desk.

"I—" Holly stopped, looked around the room and back to Adam. "You're very busy aren't you?"

"Oh, always," Adam replied cheerfully.

Holly was silent, absorbing the unpleasant implications. She folded her arms and tapped her foot. "You haven't been doing your homework before coming over to our house to play."

"Have so. I'm a morning person, anyway." Adam lounged against his desk, grinning.

Holly wagged a finger at him. "You are not. And the receptionist says you don't go out to lunch."

"Don't want to."

They eyed each other.

"What's up?" Adam continued to lean against his desk—no chair was available for Holly—extremely relaxed, considering that moments before, he had been a whirlwind of activity.

Holly deliberately rested her weight on the desk, side by side with Adam. "An anonymous philanthropist just hired us to decorate the children's wing of the hospital. He must have seen our stuff in one of the *Town Square* magazines they leave in the waiting rooms. Laurel and Ivy are thrilled and, uh, they insisted I come to invite you along, since you got to hear all about it last Sunday."

"I'd be delighted."

"But Adam!" Holly gestured at the mess around them. "You can't leave this."

Adam started to say something, but didn't. Holly suspected he was about to admit that he left it every night and cringed.

He shrugged. "I'll come in early tomorrow."

Holly walked around until she stood in front of him. "Like you do every morning?"

"Best time of the day," he said softly.

Holly gave him a long look and started for the door. "I'm going to get you some lunch. *Healthy* lunch. When I get back, I want you to tell me how I can help you."

"Thanks for the offer." Adam smiled. "I'll accept the lunch, but you're not a lawyer."

"No, but Exemplary Temps taught me how to do office busywork."

"Holly." Adam crossed the room. "You don't have to do this." His hands cupped her face and he placed a kiss on her forehead.

NO COST! NO OBLIGATION TO BUY! NO PURCHASE NECESSARY!

PLAY "LUCKY 7" AND GET AS MANY AS SIX FREE GIFTS...

HOW TO PLAY:

1. With a coin, carefully scratch off the silver box at the right. This makes you eligible to receive one or more free books, and possibly other gifts, depending on what is revealed beneath the scratch-off area.

2. You'll receive brand-new Harlequin Romance® novels. When you return this card, we'll send you the books and gifts you qualify for *absolutely free*!

3. If we don't hear from you, every month we'll send you 6 additional novels to read and enjoy. You can return them and owe nothing but if you decide to keep them, you'll pay only $2.24* per book, a savings of 26¢ each off the cover price. There is *no* extra charge for postage and handling. There are no hidden extras.

4. When you join the Harlequin Reader Service®, you'll get our monthly newsletter, as well as additional free gifts from time to time just for being a subscriber.

5. You must be completely satisfied. You may cancel at any time simply by sending us a note or a shipping statement marked "cancel" or returning any shipment to us at our cost.

This lovely Victorian pewter-finish miniature is perfect for displaying a treasured photograph— and it's yours absolutely free—when you accept our no-risk offer.

DETACH AND MAIL CARD TODAY

HARLEQUIN "NO RISK" GUARANTEE
- You're not required to buy a single book—ever!
- You must be completely satisfied or you may cancel at any time simply by sending us a note or a shipping statement marked "cancel" or returning any shipment to us at our cost. Either way, you will receive no more books; you'll have no further obligation.
- The free books and gifts you receive from this "Lucky 7" offer remain yours to keep no matter what you decide.

If offer card is missing, write to:
Harlequin Reader Service, 3010 Walden Ave., P.O. Box 1867, Buffalo, N.Y. 14269-1867

DETACH AND MAIL CARD TODAY

BUSINESS REPLY MAIL
FIRST CLASS MAIL   PERMIT NO. 717   BUFFALO, NY

POSTAGE WILL BE PAID BY ADDRESSEE

HARLEQUIN READER SERVICE
3010 WALDEN AVE
PO BOX 1867
BUFFALO NY 14240-9952

NO POSTAGE
NECESSARY
IF MAILED
IN THE
UNITED STATES

"Sure I do," Holly said as Adam released her and she hurried out the door. "I didn't tell you about the Santa suit yet."

HOLLY COUNTED IT a major achievement when she cleared the leather sofa in Adam's office after several hours of tedious work. She rewarded herself by stretching full-length on it. Her eyes drifted shut as the intercom buzzed.

"Hey, move over." Adam nudged her feet onto the floor. "I want to sit here and enjoy the thirty seconds before another load arrives."

"Adam, what are you? The garbage dump for the office?"

Adam chuckled wearily as he rubbed his temples. "I mediate nonroutine controversies and assign cases."

"You haven't assigned very many cases."

"I like to keep the difficult ones."

Holly sat up. "You're doing all the behind-the-scenes work and other lawyers are getting all the glory."

Adam rested his head on the sofa back and stared at the ceiling. "I don't want that kind of glory. I do not enjoy tearing apart the remnants of people's lives just so I get a mark in the win column. I like sitting around a table with two opposing sides and hammering out a way for everyone to get on with their lives. I've won if people resolve their differences and are still speaking to each other." Adam closed his eyes in a slow blink, then turned his head toward Holly. "Understand?"

"No."

Adam wore his bland face. When he spoke, his words were barely above a whisper. "If I'd been mediating for you, your father's estate could have been sorted out in a quarter of the time. There might even have been something left for you."

"I don't want *something,* I want it all. I'm entitled to it."

Adam shook his head. "That attitude clogs the courts and makes lawyers rich. With compromise, everybody wins."

"That's giving in, admitting you're wrong."

"You see? When people let their emotions interfere—"

"Oh, no," Holly interrupted. "I learned, right here in the glorious offices of Swinehart, Cathardy and Steele—" she threw her arms out in an all-encompassing gesture "—that emotions have no place in business."

"And you don't think anger and bitterness are emotions?"

"They're reminders."

"Great." Adam reached out and put his arm around her shoulder. "Wouldn't want you to go soft."

Holly heard the faint sarcasm in his voice and didn't care. "If I'd gone soft, we wouldn't be getting paid to decorate at the hospital tonight. But," she added, trying to lighten Adam's flat mood, "I've been known to mellow a bit."

"How?"

"I just spent the entire afternoon here with you."

"I have a feeling I'm going to pay for that in some way."

"No, no. It's an honor, really."

"Mmm." Adam absently caressed her shoulder, his eyes closed.

Just when Holly thought he had drifted off to sleep, he opened his eyes, training his blue gaze on her. "You mentioned children and a Santa suit within moments of each other."

"Oooh. You're good. I thought you missed the bit about the Santa suit."

Adam raised an eyebrow at her.

Holly stared down at her hands, finding some imperfection on her thumbnail and examining it. "It was Ivy's idea. I'll be wearing Mom's Mrs. Claus outfit and . . . ."

A dimple deepened in Adam's cheek. "Finally asking for help?"

"This isn't help, it's atmosphere." She glanced up at him, trying to gauge his reaction. He was back to the blandly pleasant lawyer again. She hated that. He did it so well. She flung her hands apart. "Ivy is...Ivy's trying to make everything like it was."

"*Ivy* is."

Holly took a deep, exasperated breath. "The children like it."

Adam nodded. "The children."

"Adam!"

"Holly?"

They stared at each other.

"Are you worried that I'll get lascivious notions at the thought of you playing Mrs. Claus to my Santa?" He leered at her.

Holly began to laugh, a deep throaty laugh. "You'll do it, won't you?"

"Ho ho ho."

"YOUR FATHER was a *big* man." Adam stared at the folds of red velvet pooling around his ankles.

"Yes," chorused three female voices. There was one Mrs. Claus, one elf and one red designer jumpsuit.

"Don't worry, Adam," fussed Holly. "No one will know when we stuff the legs into the boots.

"Ho ho."

"Adam, honey, say that with more conviction. You're the darlingest Santa we've ever had." Laurel handed him another pillow.

"Okay, ladies, that's it for the pillows. I can't bend as it is." Adam hitched the belt tighter, looking at himself in the mirror with resignation. Only the bubbling happiness of the three sisters made this worth it.

Half an hour later, as they went from room to room, Holly experienced a wide scope of emotions. There was the inevitable jerking on her heartstrings when she saw the children and their concerned parents. There was happiness and nostalgia and unexpected memories of past Christmases. She almost wished she could hand the hospital's check right back. Almost.

"These outfits remind me of the final scene in *White Christmas*," Adam said, catching their reflections in the windowed corridors of the hospital.

"That's because they're copies of the costumes in the final scene of *White Christmas*." Holly flicked her muff under Adam's nose—the only part other than his eyes not covered in whiskers.

And those eyes. Holly sighed inwardly. They'd been sending her wicked messages all evening. Most un-Santalike messages.

They passed the nurses' station. Holly was sweltering in the heavy costume and could only imagine how Adam felt. He'd been the perfect Santa. Rather than a boisterous, booming character, he'd been gentle and low-key. He talked quietly to the children who could talk; other times he simply sat next to the beds while Holly and her sisters quickly put up small twinkling trees.

It wasn't too late when they finished the children's rooms and began the large tree in the children's wing waiting room.

"The angel tree, I see," Adam said as he opened one of the boxes.

"*An* angel tree. I didn't have enough notice to save one of the others, but I think this one is better here. The angels are all different. Like the children."

"See, you are a softie." Adam took off his hat and beard. "I'd like to get out of this suit," he said, loosening his belt and removing the pillows. "Then I can help you."

"Adam . . ." Holly wanted to tell him how he'd made the evening special for her, that having him there, wearing the silly suit, had meant a lot to her. She'd just realized it herself.

"Be back in a few minutes," Adam said, and the moment was lost.

Holly watched Adam on his way down the hall. He walked with a grace her bear of a father had never had. For just a moment, the thought of her father brought hot tears to Holly's eyes. She didn't know why she was so weepy this evening.

"Got it bad, huh, Holly? Here, untangle these lights. Why did you bring so many, anyway?" Laurel handed her a snarled string of fairy lights.

"Quit jerking them out of the box and they won't tangle." Holly handed the string back to Laurel and got the rest of the lights out of the box herself.

The next time she looked for Adam, he had stopped at the nurses' station and was opening a canned soft drink.

"That looks good. You all want something to drink?" When her sisters nodded, Holly headed for the station. Several of the nurses were talking with Adam.

"... will just love it," she heard as she approached.

"It was sweet of you to do it."

Holly missed Adam's reply. One of the nurses noticed her. "Y'all did a really great job."

Holly smiled her thanks. "It was more fun than work. Please thank whoever hired us."

"Thank him yourself. He's standing right here."

Holly's eyes flew to Adam just in time to catch the slight shake of his head. She heard a soft groan from behind the desk. "Adam?" she whispered.

"Sorry. I'm just getting off a twelve-hour shift. Otherwise I wouldn't have..." The nurse shrugged.

Adam quirked a half smile at her, not certain how Holly would take this. "It's a couple of days early, but happy birthday."

"Oh, Adam." And the stoic Holly Hall burst into tears.

"I'LL MAKE SOME hot chocolate," Ivy offered as the Deck the Halls van pulled into the driveway.

"Trying to avoid unloading duties?" Laurel asked, slamming the door.

Ignoring her sisters, Holly looked up at Adam. "Can you stay? You don't really have to go in so early tomorrow, do you?"

Adam drew her closer. Holly had let Laurel drive, choosing to sit next to Adam. "Have you got any jobs tomorrow?"

"Just two. The omigosh-it's-nearly-Christmas-and-I'm-not-ready-for-it kind. And that's it. We'll do them tomorrow morning."

Adam nodded. "I'll have a cup of hot chocolate."

Ivy had the hot chocolate ready when they finished unloading the boxes. Adam followed Holly into the kitchen. She'd been quiet ever since her outburst at the hospital, content to hold his hand on the drive home. He hadn't minded.

Adam hadn't intended for the sisters to find out that he'd arranged for them to decorate the children's wing at the hospital. Holly hadn't said anything about it to Ivy and Laurel and he hoped that she wouldn't. He didn't want to change the easygoing relationship he had with them. On the other hand, he intended to disentangle Holly from her family right after Christmas.

"Where's your tree?" he asked suddenly.

"We don't get one for ourselves anymore." Ivy's voice was clipped.

"This time of year, there isn't money left for *unbudgeted frivolities*." Laurel sipped her chocolate and eyed Holly over the rim of her cup.

Adam watched as the guilt flashed across Holly's features, then turned his head to face Laurel. Laurel's gaze flicked from Holly to him, was caught and held. Her eyes, brown like Holly's, widened.

With Laurel, Adam didn't choose to be gentle. When he looked at Holly, his eyes were warm. As family, her sisters had been included in that warmth—until now. A muscle worked in his jaw and he knew his expression was hard—he intended it to be. *If you hurt Holly again,* his eyes said to a wary Laurel, *you deal with me.* The look on his face left no doubt that the experience would be an unpleasant one.

His eyes briefly left Laurel's to direct a piercing glance at Ivy, who blushed, then went back to Laurel. Adam reached for his mug of hot chocolate and took a sip. Laurel set hers on the table as the slight trembling in her hands became perceptible.

Holly noticed nothing. She was embarrassed and furious with her sisters and took a few moments to compose herself. She fervently hoped that Adam would not interpret their remarks as a hint that he buy their Christmas tree.

"Usually we're too tired to decorate our own, anyway." Holly dredged up a smile. "But this year, why not?"

"Ivy and I'll buy one after the last job tomorrow," Laurel said hastily.

"I'd like to come by and see what sort of tree the professionals choose for themselves," Adam said, finishing his chocolate and getting to his feet.

Holly laughed. "Whatever is left over."

"I could come by your office tomorrow after we finish," she offered as she walked Adam to his car. "Help you with some of the paperwork. Then you could have dinner with us."

"Very tempting," Adam said softly, admiring her face in the moonlight.

Holly shivered and wrapped her arms around herself.

"Let me." Adam opened his coat and held it around her while she snuggled against his heart.

"Thank you for my birthday present," she said softly, not wanting to disturb the stillness of the night. "It was wonderful." She looked up at him. "You are wonderful."

Her mouth was only inches away from his and he closed the distance quickly. Their lips were cold, and Holly and Adam drew apart, laughing, before melting together once more.

Holly was surrounded by Adam, by his warmth and scent. She worked her arms out of the cocoon of his coat to wrap them around his neck as she pressed herself closer.

He tasted of chocolate.

"Holly." He filled her name with all the pent-up yearning he'd felt for weeks. She'd warned him she didn't want to become involved and he hadn't believed her for a while. A very short while. Just until he'd spent long stretches working next to her, learning all about her. He lived for moments like this one, when she seemed to want him as much as he wanted her. He'd gone so slowly, never cornering her into choosing between Deck the Halls and Adam Markland. He'd tried to fit into her life. Now he was going to find out how successful he'd been.

"Holly," he said again, his breath warming her face. "I'd enjoy a quiet evening with you—alone," he added, deciding to drop some early hints. "But I'm only going into the office for a couple of hours tomorrow. I've got an afternoon flight home to Boston."

"Boston?" Holly searched his face. "You won't be here for Christmas?"

The dismayed surprise on her face was an encouraging sign. "I'm spending Christmas at home with my family. My brother and sister will be there with their kids." It occurred to him that she might ask him to stay. He could; after all, he'd just been home for Thanksgiving. No, if Holly was ever going to think about him and what he meant to her, she needed time alone. Christmas was that time.

"Of course." Holly recovered quickly and gently pushed herself out of Adam's circle of warmth. "I forgot that you aren't a free agent." She shivered.

"Get back in the house," he directed softly. "I'll drop by tomorrow on my way to the airport with something to put under your tree."

A Christmas present! Holly had thought she'd have two more days. She'd always been a last-minute shopper, finding that her impulse buys were usually the best. Besides, she never knew until Christmas Eve how much money she could spend.

This year, she had money, but no time.

"DO YOU THINK he'll like it?" Holly looked at Laurel, panic in her expression.

"It's real cute, Holly," Laurel drawled.

"He'll hate it." Holly dropped her head on the kitchen table beside the small box she was measuring for paper.

"I don't know," Laurel picked up the little glass bear. "You've decorated it real nice."

"Oh, cut it out." Holly snatched the bear back and polished off Laurel's fingerprints.

"It *is* Steuben glass. You've still got some taste, I see," Laurel muttered.

"What'll I do?" Holly wailed. "He'll be here any minute."

"I could help you select a nice tie."

"I couldn't give Adam a tie! It's too…impersonal. Bears are special to us."

"Special to us?" Laurel repeated with heavy emphasis. "Is there an 'us'?"

"I don't know." Holly studied the little bear. "I saw this and it reminded me of the night we met. You remember—"

"Yes, and I'd rather forget. I don't mean Adam," Laurel added when she saw the look on Holly's face.

"We tied these little ribbons around all those bears Bloomie got for us." Holly smiled to herself as she placed the bear back in its nest of tissue paper.

"How sweet."

"I thought so."

Laurel drifted toward the refrigerator, opened it and peered inside. "Holly," she said, extracting an apple and closing the door. "Has it occurred to you that Adam isn't a *sweet* man?"

"No, it hasn't." Holly ripped off tape with a snap.

"Honey, you've hooked more man than you know." Laurel gestured to the glass door behind Holly. "Let me know if you decide to throw him back."

"What?" As Holly stared at Laurel, she heard the slam of a car door and barely had enough time to stash the wrapping paper in the pantry. "Stick this under the tree," she said, thrusting the box at Laurel as she watched Adam's approach.

"You came around back," Holly said, a little breathlessly, when she opened the door.

Adam flashed her a smile. "Lunchtime?"

"Uh—" Holly looked around the kitchen "—we were trying to get the tree up before you got here." True, but she neglected to tell him that their morning jobs took longer than scheduled because she was Christmas shopping instead of helping.

"How about a turkey sandwich?" she offered, trying to ignore the large red-and-gold package Adam held.

"Sounds fine, but lead me to the tree first."

Holly led Adam through the house into the living room.

"Oh, no." It slipped out before she could stop it.

"Hi!" Ivy grinned at them from her perch on the ladder. "Well Adam, we've done our part." She finished tying the last of at least two dozen bunches of mistletoe and hopped down. "Think I'll go into the kitchen and start lunch." She gave Adam an exaggerated wink in passing.

"Think I'll go with you." Laurel and her husky laugh followed.

"That's an interesting shade of pink," Adam commented, tilting Holly's chin.

"I can't believe they're so obvious."

Adam laughed, took her hand and led her to the tree. "I rather like it," he said and positioned her under one of the bunches.

"They poked holes in the ceiling," Holly grumbled before Adam claimed his kiss.

Afterward, she didn't mind the holes at all.

"Now, about this tree..." Adam regarded the jumble in front of them.

"We each have our favorite ornaments," Holly explained.

"It isn't coordinated."

"We like it that way."

"Good." Adam sat on the carpet and nudged the red-and-gold package under the tree. It joined one small silver box.

Holly sank down next to him, besieged by nerves.

"Tomorrow's Christmas Eve." Adam leaned back against a chair, totally at ease. Although he didn't smile, his eyes held a secret amusement. "Do you want to open your present now, or wait?"

"I—" Holly broke off as she considered whether she wanted to prolong the suspense or get the embarrassment and the explanations over with.

"Personally, I like to watch people's faces when they open my gifts." His dimples deepened, but he still wasn't actually smiling. The wretch was *laughing* at her!

"Here." She grabbed the silver box and shoved it into his lap.

"Here, yourself." Adam thunked the large box on Holly's legs.

Her heart pounded. He'd think her present was goofy.

She was convinced that she was about to open a five-or ten-pound box of chocolates. She hoped they were Godiva. If she got fat, it wasn't going to be on cheap chocolate.

She couldn't stand his staring at her, and plucked at the sticky tape. "Let's open them at the same time." She had magnified this out of all proportion. They were just friends, for heaven's sake.

She couldn't look at him. He was obviously of the paper-ripping school, while she liked to unwrap slowly.

The tearing sound stopped. Holly sneaked a quick peek as Adam took off the box lid.

Hearing his delighted laugh, she exhaled. Adam crawled over to her. "Look—his bow is crooked." He retied it. "Brings back memories."

"It's supposed to."

The blazing look Adam gave her made Holly catch her breath.

"Open yours," he urged softly.

Holly ripped the rest of the paper. Inside the box was a framed copy of the *Town Square* magazine with their cover.

"Adam!" Holly reached up and threw her arms around him in a great hug. "Thanks," she whispered softly.

She leaned against him, admiring the cover. "I wish you weren't going back to Boston for Christmas, but I know you want to be with your family."

It took all Adam's self-control not to cancel his flight instantly. He'd better leave now, while he could still convince himself to go.

He squeezed Holly's shoulders briefly. "I'm going to take a rain check on the turkey sandwich. I need to get to the airport. Walk me to the door and stop under some mistletoe on the way.''

Giggling, Holly hopscotched out of the living room and into the foyer. Adam followed and they broke in as many bunches of mistletoe as they could.

"Your car's around back," Holly reminded him.

"I know. I want to say goodbye in private."

Holly smiled wickedly and planted herself under a particularly large bunch of Ivy's mistletoe. When Adam dutifully bent his head, she locked her arms behind his neck and sinuously pressed herself against him. Extremely satisfied with herself as she felt a shudder pass through his body, she backed him against the front door and began to undo the buttons of his plaid shirt.

Holly trailed kisses after her fingers, enjoying the feel of the softly curling hair on his chest.

"Holly!" She heard the hoarse rumble in his chest and stopped abruptly as two strong hands firmly set her away. "No more games." Adam closed his eyes and took a deep breath.

Holly was ashamed when she realized how affected Adam was by her caresses.

"Sorry," she mumbled, quickly buttoning his shirt once more. "I guess I was hoping you'd decide to stay."

The corner of Adam's mouth lifted in a half smile and he managed a credible drawl. "Holly, honey, I'll be back."

CHAPTER SEVEN

WHEN WAS HE COMING BACK? How could she have let him leave without telling her when he'd be back?

Boston. It might as well have been the moon. He'd only been gone two days, but it was Christmas and Holly missed him. She thought she'd handled everything so coolly, being very straightforward about her intentions. No time for relationships.

How was she supposed to know he'd take her at her word?

She should be scheduling their tree dismantlings. At least that's what she told Laurel and Ivy when she escaped to her room after the Christmas dinner dishes were done. Ivy would spend the rest of the day watching football and Laurel was doing who knew what. Probably eating.

She ought to have done the books and typed the statements by now. Instead, she'd spent all day mooning about Adam Markland. This was ridiculous. Maybe if she went downstairs to the office, she'd get some work done.

ADAM CHECKED HIS WATCH, calculating how soon he could break away and call Holly. He had decided that he would— a quick Christmas greeting. He wanted her to think about him, after all.

His father gently cleared his throat. "You've been rather tight-lipped about the cases you're handling at Steele's, Adam."

Adam glanced quickly toward the head of the table and met his father's querying look. "Testing me, Dad?"

"Not at all." The elder Markland blotted his mouth with a snowy damask napkin. "Confidentiality is understood. But there is nothing ethically wrong with consulting your colleagues for another opinion."

His family called it consulting, but it was nonstop talking shop. The only way Adam could avoid it was to play trains with his nephews.

"Yes, and we'd like some tips on handling bankruptcy cases," his brother said with what Adam knew was complete sincerity.

That was the problem. His family lived and breathed law, celebrating victories and agonizing over defeats.

There were more victories than defeats. A client didn't hire one Markland—he hired all of them, with their combined specialities and driving desire to win at any cost.

"I'm mediating my cases." There was silence around the dinner table. Adam looked into the faces of his mother, father, brother and sister and sighed inwardly. His brother-in-law and sister-in-law looked at him pityingly. They were also lawyers.

"You mean you haven't won any." Stephanie Markland Brandt's blue eyes regarded his knowingly.

Adam bit back a harsh retort. "Our definition of winning isn't the same. Don't worry—business is good. I'm not starving." He reached for his coffee.

Four pairs of Markland-blue eyes assessed him, and he responded with the pleasantly bland face Holly hated.

Shouting erupted in the kitchen. "I'll go referee," Adam said, glad to leave the dining room. It would give them the chance to talk about him, but he didn't care.

"Tell you what," Adam said as he served his boisterous nephews and niece their Christmas cake, "Come upstairs when you finish these and we'll play trains."

Figuring he had about five minutes, Adam dashed up the back staircase and into the upstairs library.

The phone on her desk rang loudly, startling Holly. Her heart began to pound and she forced herself to let the phone ring twice before she pounced on it. "Hello?"

"Merry Christmas, Holly."

Holly grinned like an idiot. "Merry Christmas, Adam."

She knew he was smiling, too; she could practically hear it. A few seconds slipped by while every rational thought escaped Holly's mind.

"Do you miss me?" Adam prompted.

"Of course we miss you! Laurel and Ivy haven't forgiven me for not convincing you to stay. We got so used to having you around." Holly paused, conscious of how awful that sounded.

"I asked if *you* miss me."

Holly heard shouting in the background. "I—"

"Uncle Adam!" It echoed right in her ear, along with Adam's laughter. "The troops found me. I promised them we'd play trains— Hey! Don't jump on me—"

The phone crashed to the floor and Holly could hear laughing and shrieking. A breathless Adam finally retrieved the telephone. "Holly, I've got to go. Talk to you later."

She still didn't know when he'd be back. It would serve her right if he *didn't* come back. Why should he rush away from his family? At the very least she should have admitted how much she missed him.

Work. That would take her mind off Adam Markland. Holly scanned her client list, checking for those who had scheduled a tree-dismantling in advance. Not one for December 26.

She threw down her pen. How could she concentrate? Her life was a mess.

No, it wasn't. She had never been as financially stable as she was this season. She hugged her knees to her chest in the great leather chair that had been her father's. Burrowing down, she could still smell the horrible cigars he used to smoke in here after dinner. Holly inhaled deeply, then straightened, reaching for her pen, which had bounced across the massive oak desk.

Financial stability. Security. She could relax, pull back some, right?

Okay, so exactly how much of this season's success did she owe to Adam? As long as she couldn't stop thinking about him, she might as well find out.

Holly unfolded her scheduling calendar and began to list the jobs Adam had worked on. Grinning to herself, she decided to allocate minimum wage to his work hours, which had been nearly every evening and every Saturday since they'd met.

She'd been selfish, she admitted, remembering the late nights and the condition of his office.

Holly gritted her teeth when she finished calculating Adam's work hours. Suspecting was one thing, seeing it confirmed was something else. She pushed herself out of the leather chair and found last year's records.

No wonder this had been a good year. Holly fought back tears of censure. Look at the jobs she'd scheduled from the middle of the month on. Twice as many as before. They couldn't have handled the work load without him. She had calculated Adam's unpaid help into their job times.

She added in the profits from the hospital job. Feeling masochistic at this point, she figured in an arbitrary amount for the pizzas and deli food Adam always brought with him.

Holly felt horrible. She must be in love.

"When have I had time to fall in love?" she asked aloud. When people fell in love, they saw it coming. They went out to eat, they danced, they took long walks together. They went to movies, to the symphony and a few charity functions, right? They prepared for it—nurtured it. They allowed it to come into their lives.

This couldn't be love. She wasn't ready for love. She had to put Ivy through college first.

In an unreasonable panic, Holly began to feel angry. How dared Adam allow her to fall in love with him?

A night's sleep improved Holly's outlook. Work should make it even better. Some people, somewhere, wanted to get rid of their tree today. She was going to call until she found them.

Holly had her hand on the telephone when it rang. Startled, she jerked her hand away, then laughed. "Deck the Halls," she answered.

"Oh, which sister have I got?"

"Holly."

"Holly, dear, I need help. It's dreadful, but it's actually an honor, but a terrible imposition, but how could I turn them down? Where else could they go?"

The disjointed ramble in the cigarette-hoarsened voice could only come from Claudia Fitzhugh. "How can we help, Mrs. Fitzhugh?" Holly asked, trying to infuse her voice with reassuring calm and not giving in to an urge to laugh.

"Oh, I knew I could count on you, Holly, dear. You're just like your mother and I could always count on her when things got in a tangle."

"What's wrong?" Holly prompted, becoming impatient.

"Martha is in such a tizzy about it all. She accused me of being jealous, which is true, because I'm a human being and there isn't a person alive who wouldn't be, and after all, I'm Bernard's sister, but just because I'm not invited doesn't mean I can't tell her she shouldn't have canceled everything even if she isn't going to be here."

"Mrs. Fitzhugh!" Holly managed to interject when the woman stopped for breath. "I've been out of touch for a while and I don't know what you're talking about."

"Oh, dear. I think I'm having a New Year's Eve reception in my home."

"You don't know?"

"Well, I'm not having it if I can't make the proper arrangements. It's the Music League's reception for the symphony musicians and the Green Room donors."

"The one after the New Year's Eve pops concert? Mother and Dad used to go."

"My sister-in-law, Martha Steele, was having it this year. She got a call last week from the White House, and she and Bernard have been invited to a New Year's Eve gala with the president! It was a telephoned invitation," Mrs Fitzhugh stressed, "so there must have been a cancellation."

Holly bit back a smile.

"And the silly woman only tells me this morning! She *canceled* the caterer and the room designer! I called immediately, but of course they were booked." Mrs. Fitzhugh let out an exasperated breath. "And having Mr. Kelly was such a coup. Now, dear, please tell me you aren't booked for New Year's Eve, too?"

Holly's heart began to pound. "We don't do food, Mrs. Fitzhugh."

"I realize that, dear, but when you did my tree, you did say you wanted to expand into social events. And, frankly, the better-known names will already be hired."

"Mrs. Fitzhugh, Deck the Halls would be thrilled to decorate your home. What about a budget and a theme?" Holly flipped through the pages of her phone book, looking for Mrs. Bloom's number.

"Whatever you've got." Mrs. Fitzhugh was realistic when she needed to be.

Holly hung up the phone and let out a yell that brought Ivy and Laurel running.

She spent the rest of the week happily preparing for the party. She wanted to share her good news with Adam, but he didn't call, which was fine with her. She didn't have time to be in love, anyway.

Late in the afternoon of the thirtieth, the doorbell rang.

Holly's hands stilled as one of her sisters answered it. A moment passed, and she continued slowly making a bow out of silver netting.

Adam appeared in the workroom doorway and leaned a leather-clad shoulder against it. His cheekbones wore a ruddy stain, due to the recent cold snap. The lock of hair, still untamed, fell across his forehead.

Holly wanted to stand up and throw herself into his arms. But he'd been gone a week and had only called her once for about two minutes. She didn't know what to think. "Hello, Adam," she said, trying to sound nonchalant.

"Hello, yourself. I just got back."

"Did you have a good time?" Couldn't she come up with something better than that?

"Yes, I did," Adam answered politely. "I'd like to take you out tomorrow night."

"That's New Year's Eve."

"I know. People go out on New Year's Eve all the time." There was amusement in his voice.

"We're booked this New Year's, isn't that great?" In trying to sound enthusiastic, which she was, Holly overdid it.

"No." His blue eyes turned stormy.

Holly ignored him. "Claudia Fitzhugh hired us to decorate for the symphony's New Year's Eve reception. Isn't that fantastic? Think of the contacts we'll make."

Adam crossed his arms. "It's after Christmas, Holly."

"I know," she answered quietly.

"I thought things were going to slow down after Christmas."

"They did."

Adam watched as her fingers fumbled with the netting, taking longer with this bow than any of the others. "Is your presence required for the duration of the party?"

Holly gave up on the bow. "Adam, it's our *first* society function. We have the opportunity to make incredible contacts."

"I thought your family was a member of the upper echelon."

"Was. The upper echelon has a short memory."

Adam's stern expression made Holly uncomfortable. "Mrs. Fitzhugh invited us to stay. Laurel and Ivy will be there, too. Laurel needs your tree skirt to wear." Holly tried a light laugh.

Adam's blue eyes were unreadable. "How many other parties are you doing?"

"None . . . yet."

"Black tie?"

"Of course."

"Of course." Adam turned, obviously leaving.

"Adam—wait."

He turned back, raising an eyebrow.

"I missed you," Holly said, barely above a whisper.

Adam's lips curved in the smallest of smiles, but he shook his head slightly and left.

"YOU NEED SOME PEACE and quiet," Adam said as he opened Holly's front door.

"Everything looked all right at the party, didn't it?"

"Yes," he reassured Holly smilingly. "It was perfect."

"Well, not perfect—"

"Holly."

She looked at him, recognizing the warning note in his voice.

"It's a new year. We're alone, with each other, and I have a plate of party goodies and a bottle of champagne. Getting some ideas?" He nodded his head toward the family room.

Holly grabbed two glasses and followed him, sitting on the sofa as he opened the champagne.

"To the future."

"It's going to be great, isn't it, Adam?" Holly set her champagne on the coffee table and leaned back.

Adam didn't kiss her the way she'd hoped. Perhaps she'd better make the first move.

He held a finger to her lips. "Not just yet. Are you only after my body, or will you respect me in the morning?"

Holly was surprised into a laugh. "Adam, you lunatic, kiss me."

Adam's even white teeth tugged at his lip as he shook his head. "Answer."

"You're serious!" Holly said, amazed.

"I have a right to know." She obviously didn't understand, so he elaborated. "I told you before that I don't go in for flings. Where are we headed?"

"Adam," Holly protested, running her hand through her curls, "it's only a kiss."

"Is it?" Adam cupped her chin with his hand and pressed his lips against hers.

At least that was the physical description of what he did. But how it *felt* was something else altogether. Being confronted with her feelings for Adam frightened Holly. He would start making demands—already his lips were demanding a response from her. Her blood became liquid fire, making her achingly aware of him.

She gasped when he broke the kiss.

"You see?" he asked, softly triumphant, mouth slanted in a half smile.

Holly was too bemused to answer.

"You can slow down now, can't you, Holly? I'm not asking you to quit work so you can be at my beck and call. Just make room for me—for *us* in your life."

Holly wound her arms around his neck. "I love you, Adam."

To her astonishment, a look of pain and anger flashed across his face.

"But you're not *in* love with me."

Before she could reply, Holly heard the unmistakable sounds of the front door opening. She stared at Adam's tight face. "What's the difference?"

"You haven't been alone with me long enough to find out," she heard him say as Laurel and Ivy burst into the room.

"This has been the most wonderful evening!" Laurel proclaimed, her eyes bright and her cheeks flushed.

"Champagne will do that to you." Holly was glad of their company. What was with Adam? She'd just told him she loved him, for heaven's sake!

"Not champagne—a man."

"Who?"

"Bart King. He's a member of the Southwest Film Commission and I think he can help me in my career."

"What, they want Deck the Halls to decorate for some films?" Holly leaned forward eagerly, missing the bitter smile on Adam's face.

"Holly, honey, he couldn't care less about Deck the Halls."

"What help could he possibly be, then?"

Laurel glanced at Ivy. "My acting career."

"Your acting career," Holly repeated immediately, unaware she had done so. "You don't have an acting career."

"I'm hoping to change all that."

Ivy prudently remained quiet.

"You don't have any experience," Holly pointed out.

"Don't you think this has been one big act for the last five years? Living here—" Laurel gestured all around them "—with the impeccably decorated front rooms and the rest of the house gutted? Sharing our clothes, bringing home all those sugar packets, crackers and doggie bags from the restaurants? Gorging ourselves at salad bars so there would *be* doggie bags? Even Mama was acting." Laurel reached out and tugged at the necklace Holly wore. "Keeping up appearances has been one long act, hasn't it?"

Holly took a deep breath. "It is cheaper for us to live in this house than anywhere else. If you'd remember any of your business training, you'd know that. The real-estate market is in the toilet and this house is paid for. All we do is pay taxes, which are deductible. Rent isn't."

"Okay, okay. You probably don't remember, but when I was at SMU, I loved my drama classes. It's what I want to do. I think things could finally begin to happen for me."

Holly turned to Adam. "It's the champagne talking."

"Holly." Laurel was so intense she forgot to drawl the "honey." "I'm almost twenty-five. I want a job of my own—"

"Deck the Halls is better than a job! We own the company."

Laurel changed tactics. "We've finally got some money. Ivy is going to college, so you'll need to hire someone, anyway. It's a new year. New beginnings."

"How could you even *think* of wasting your business degree after all we've sacrificed for it!" Holly's patience was gone.

Laurel looked as if she'd been slapped. "You don't need a business degree to rent Christmas-tree decorations."

"There is a lot to running your own business."

"How would I know?" Laurel asked caustically. "*You* keep the records; You make the decisions. You didn't even trust me to decorate a tree by myself until this year."

"You can't earn your living acting!"

"I want to try!"

The room went horribly quiet.

"I can't allow it, Laurel," Holly said unyieldingly.

"It's her life, Holly," said Adam's calm voice behind her.

"You, too?" Holly was stung. "She doesn't know anything about acting."

"She can learn."

"She'll ruin her life. I didn't work this hard so she could waste everything on a whim." How could the man she loved take Laurel's side?

"This isn't a whim," Laurel said.

"It's her life," Adam repeated. "And she's old enough to know what she wants."

Laurel nodded regally. "Thank you, Adam."

Holly's lip quivered and no one was fooled into thinking it was from impending tears.

Laurel put a hand on Holly's shoulder and Holly shrugged it off. "Holly, nothing will happen right away. I just wanted you to know, because I won't be spending as much time with Deck the Halls. Mr. King offered me a job as a receptionist, so I'll work there and save money for acting classes."

"Thank you for telling me," Holly said icily.

Laurel stood there a moment more, then she and Ivy left the room.

Holly whirled on Adam. "Traitor!"

"Now who's the actress?"

"I know." Holly squinted at him. "You took Laurel's side because you think I'll give up the business then."

"Holly..." he began with exasperation, but she ignored him.

"Nothing can interfere with Deck the Halls. I won't let it. I will do anything to make it succeed." Holly shook her head. "Anything."

"Thus proving you aren't in love with me." Adam's voice was cold. "You'd sacrifice us to Deck the Halls. But I wouldn't choose my job over you because nothing is as important as what we have together—what we *could* have together."

"Being a success is *important* to me, Adam," Holly said urgently. Why wouldn't he understand?

Adam's eyes searched her face. "You're trying to be a success at Laurel's expense."

"That's not true," Holly lashed out, hurt at Adam's betrayal. "For two years, Ivy and I worked so Laurel could get her degree. Now she wants to throw it all back in our faces."

"Let her go, Holly." Adam reached out to caress her cheek, but Holly batted his hand away. He sighed. "People have different definitions of success. For me, achieving happiness is success."

"If I'm a success, I'm happy," Holly shot back.

"Then I'm sorry for you."

"I don't want your pity!" she snapped.

At Adam's silence, Holly began to feel uncomfortable.

"You remind me very much of my family," he commented at last. "It's money, power and winning. Nothing else matters."

That was easy for him to say. He'd never been poor or powerless. "You'd better believe it."

Adam looked directly into her eyes. "You don't mean that."

Holly met his gaze unflinchingly. "Oh, yes, I do."

Now Adam's eyes mirrored Holly's feeling of betrayal. "Then we have nothing more to say to each other, do we?"

CHAPTER EIGHT

"I DON'T WANT to go to SMU," Ivy stated flatly. "It's too expensive. I had no idea you were trying to save up that much money." She followed Holly into their office.

Why were both her sisters being so unreasonable all of a sudden? Holly wondered, tired from a day of tree dismantling and decorating for a client's dinner party. "Actually, if you live at home, it won't cost that much more than going to a state school." Holly sat back in her father's leather chair, unconsciously echoing a posture he'd assumed many times.

"Laurel got *her* degree from a state school. She didn't finish at SMU and—"

"And she's been upset ever since."

"I'm not Laurel. I'm not the sorority type," Ivy said. "I know our whole family went to SMU, but I don't want to. You should be glad—my plan's cheaper. I'm going to register at the college next week," she said resolutely.

Holly gave up. "If you change your mind about SMU, let me know. We've booked some parties for January. Little ones, like tonight, but it's a start."

"Have you and Adam made up yet?" Ivy asked.

Holly shook her head.

"Why not? You and Laurel have." Ivy handed Holly the phone. "Call him and take him with you when you go check on things tonight. He'll add to the decor."

Holly snatched the phone from Ivy and glared until her unrepentant sister left the room.

It didn't help that Ivy was right. She owed Adam an apology. She'd overreacted just because he disagreed with her.

Holly slowly punched out Adam's office number.

"Markland." Adam's voice was impersonal.

She squeezed her eyes shut. "Adam, it's Holly. I'm sorry. Laurel and I made up. Mama's diamonds and I are going out to check on a dinner party we did today. If you and your tux would like to come with us, I'll pick you up at seven. We'll stay there during cocktails and then we could get coffee or dinner or something."

There was a silence of several heartbeats—interminable to Holly. It made her realize how much she hoped Adam wasn't the kind of man who carried grudges.

"I think I'll choose the something," she heard Adam say at last.

In the end, they did have dinner, in a chain restaurant where they were overdressed.

"What's the story behind those?" Adam tugged at Holly's necklace, mimicking Laurel's gesture on New Year's Eve.

"You mean Laurel's reference during her dramatic scene?" Holly swirled the coffee in her cup before answering. "Dad bought Mama this necklace. It was her only piece of 'important' jewelry."

Adam raised his eyebrows. "She didn't need anything else."

"She didn't want anything else." Holly bit her lip and went on. "I tried to sell the diamonds and replace them with fakes before the auction." She looked at Adam defiantly. "We needed money for lawyers. Someone had to fight for us before everything was taken away. But guess what?"

Adam watched the bitterness cross Holly's face and tried to imagine how he would have reacted if his world had fallen apart when he was only twenty-two. "Do you think that necklace might be a copy? It isn't unusual to have copies made for insurance reasons. There could be a real one somewhere.''

''That's what we thought, but it appears Mama had been selling diamonds out of it for a long time. We found...papers.'' Holly gestured expressively. ''I guess things weren't going well in Dad's business.''

She fingered the necklace. ''Anyway,'' she said, lightening the mood, ''I'm making this black dress and the diamonds my signature look—like Lillie Langtry. I'll stop in during parties and eventually everyone will recognize a Deck the Halls design.''

Adam raised his coffee cup. ''To new ventures.''

IT BECAME A ROUTINE that on a party night they went out after Holly's appearance. It wasn't like any relationship Adam had ever had before. The barrier of Holly's responsibilities still came between them, frustrating him enormously. At least, he had to acknowledge they were spending time together—without her entire family looking on.

''My social life has improved markedly,'' he commented one evening. ''I kind of miss the trees, though.''

He poured Holly a glass of red table wine. They'd found a small Italian restaurant they now thought of as ''theirs.'' It reeked unashamedly of garlic and tomatoes and fresh baked loaves of crusty bread. They rarely ate a complete meal, having nibbled at parties, but Holly immediately became addicted to the oversize mugs of cappuccino, topped with an extraordinary amount of whipped cream.

''You miss all that work, huh?'' Holly dipped her spoon into the whipped cream. ''We've still got one tree left to take down.''

Adam raised his eyebrows in mock horror. ''It's January!''

At her happy face and throaty laughter, Adam ached with a sweet yearning. "It's Mrs. Fitzhugh's," Holly was saying. She left town right after New Year's and just got back. I'm taking it down tomorrow morning."

"So you are slowing down a bit." It was time to push their relationship forward. During his week in Boston at Christmas, Adam realized the only way to keep Holly from thinking about her sisters or her company would be to take her away from them. Not forever, just a weekend. A weekend for the two of them.

"A bit," Holly replied cautiously. "We have to do inventory and get rid of damaged ornaments, and check our books and—"

"Come away with me." Adam reached across the table and held both her hands in his.

"I can't," Holly protested automatically.

"You can. For a weekend. I'll plan everything."

Holly gazed into Adam's brilliant blue eyes and was lost.

His voice was quietly mesmerizing. "You won't have to think. You won't have to do anything. I want to take care of you—just for a weekend. Let your soul heal."

Holly closed her eyes. "When?"

It was barely a whisper, but Adam caught his breath. Holly opened her eyes and looked at him with so much longing, his hands began to shake. He released hers before she noticed.

"The last weekend of the month," he said with such certainty that Holly asked why.

"Where's your optimism?" Adam scolded her gently. "Deck the Halls will be booked for Valentine Day. I'm allowing plenty of time."

The next morning, a dreamy fog enveloped Holly as she tackled Mrs. Fitzhugh's tree. She suspected that Adam would have been gratified, if he'd been there to see it.

Her daydreams shattered at the sound of Mrs. Fitzhugh's scream.

Holly scrambled down the stepladder and raced into the study, where Mrs. Fitzhugh sat at a cherrywood escritoire, clutching her heart.

"No, no," Mrs. Fitzhugh moaned. She held a letter crumpled in one hand.

"Mrs. Fitzhugh!" The matron turned to her and Holly was alarmed at the gray tinge in her face. "I'm calling an ambulance."

"No!" Mrs. Fitzhugh visibly composed herself. "This has never happened to me before and now twice in one month... Martha is completely insane."

She handed the letter to Holly. "This probably came the day we left. I should have had our mail forwarded."

Holly recognized the pale green engraved notepaper instantly. Mr. John Kelly, Event Designer, regretted that he would be unable to keep his commitment to the Ballet Guild's Winter Ball due to his hiring by the Heart Foundation for its annual Valentine's Heart Ball.

"Martha and I had words," Mrs. Fitzhugh explained. "The committee and I were shocked at her behavior over the New Year's Eve reception. I expressed my concern at her unreliability, and she resigned as chairman of the Winter Ball. I, of course, was elected to replace her. And now this."

Holly leaned against one of the floral chintz chairs. "She hired him out from under you."

Mrs. Fitzhugh pulled a check for five hundred dollars out of the envelope. "His donation to a worthy cause," she said dryly. "Oh, you can hardly blame the man. Our ball is more select, but he'll get better exposure at the Heart event. Diseases are always more popular than the arts."

"I can do it." Holly took a deep breath. "Deck the Halls will do the Winter Ball, Mrs. Fitzhugh. We'll donate our services to the Ballet Guild."

"Oh, Holly, dear." Mrs. Fitzhugh smiled and shook her head. "You are so like your mother. Much too generous. I can't let you."

"How much time have I got?"

Mrs. Fitzhugh pressed her lips together. "Less than three weeks," she said crisply. "The ball is the twenty-ninth, the last weekend of the month."

The date jarred Holly's memory. She had something scheduled. Well, whatever it was, she'd cancel. This, so close to the New Year's symphony party, was a gift from fate. Fate, which had treated her horribly, was making up for lost time.

"Please, Mrs. Fitzhugh."

Mrs. Fitzhugh gazed at the determined woman before her. "Sit down, Holly," she said, all traces of flighty society matron gone. "I'm going to be very frank. You don't have the experience and you're not going to get it at my ball." She went on, softening her words. "We start planning a year in advance. We've been working with Mr. Kelly for weeks, contacting florists to donate flowers, underwriters for caterers, door prizes, the printers—"

"You won't be able to find a big-name decorator," Holly interrupted flatly. "They don't have enough time to start from scratch, and they're not about to link their name with anything less than successful."

"There you go!" Mrs. Fitzhugh flung up her hands. "If a professional can't do it—"

"*I* am a professional, Mrs. Fitzhugh. And I won't be starting from scratch."

"What do you mean?" Mrs. Fitzhugh was quick to grasp the lifeline Holly threw her.

"John Kelly isn't stupid. There's going to be publicity over this. Now, if I were Mr. Kelly, I would hope that you and your committee plan to keep his defection quiet so you'll still sell tickets."

Holly had Mrs. Fitzhugh's complete attention. "Go on."

"I'll pay a call on Mr. Kelly," Holly said, her mind working furiously. "He'll cooperate and give me his lists and discuss his plans in return for stories about how helpful he's been."

"And if he doesn't?"

"After several articles about how he backed out at the last minute, do you think anyone will ever hire him again?"

Mrs. Fitzhugh hesitated, obviously wanting to believe Holly.

"Would *you*?" Holly asked, pressing her point.

"It could ruin you."

Holly smiled. "Or it could send me right to the top."

Mrs. Fitzhugh studied Holly a moment longer. "So help me, I think you might just do it." A sly smile curved her lips. "Martha will be very annoyed."

Her sisters weren't home when Holly breezed in after her meeting with John Kelly. In her office, she began to schedule what had to be done and who was going to do it. When her sisters finally came in from who knew where, she was ready.

"Have you lost your mind?" Laurel snapped. "We can't do it. Certainly not in three weeks."

"Not by ourselves, no. But I've got a list of florists and caterers and others who are donating to the ball. There's a committee to oversee everything. We'll coordinate and do the decor."

"But Holly, my classes begin that week," Ivy protested.

"We can do this!" Holly insisted. "Can't you two see that this is the chance we've prayed for? We'll never have to waste our time on small jobs again. We can hire help. We won't have to struggle—we'll hire Exemplary Temporaries for a switch!"

"I've started drama classes," Laurel announced quietly.

"What is the matter with you two?" Holly stared in disbelief. "Don't you understand? This is it, our big chance!"

Both of her sisters sat in the office and stared back at her stonily. "Our chance for what?" Laurel asked.

Holly couldn't believe they didn't see the possibilities. "To make a lot of money," she said distinctly.

"How much are they paying you?" Laurel asked quickly.

Holly took a deep breath. "Nothing. I'm donating our services."

"Forget it, Holly." Laurel stood up. "You can donate *your* services."

"You could have asked first," Ivy said, preparing to follow Laurel.

"There wasn't time. Listen to me." Holly hurried to the door to keep them from leaving. "I'm doing this for the contacts. The Winter Ball is big news. It gets national coverage." Holly emphasized the last two words and saw interest in Laurel's eyes.

"That's right, it does," she mused, looking fixedly over Holly's shoulder.

"Now do you understand? People all over the country will hear about Deck the Halls. You two can help me and we'll make this the best Winter Ball Dallas has ever seen, or I'll do what I can by myself. Either way, we'll be noticed."

Ivy and Laurel exchanged glances. Ivy shrugged.

"Okay," Laurel said slowly, "but the next time you get the chance of a lifetime, check with us first."

"I will, I promise." Holly hugged them both. "You won't regret this, you'll see."

The days slipped by, with Holly spending most of her time on the telephone. She redid the theme. There was no way she planned to use a secondhand theme. She did like Mr. Kelly's idea of covering the ballroom in white silk, though. The room at the Landreth was heavily ornate, decorated in multihued reds. A huge quilted hanging, glorifying the Alamo, was displayed on the back wall.

Finding that much silk was a problem. Holly called a number of fabric mills to locate the hundreds of yards needed. All wanted a deposit.

Holly had just hung up the phone after talking to a sales rep at one of the mills. She was going to have to buy some and rent a lot. But she couldn't spend thousands of dollars on draping the walls without considering the rest of the room.

"Holly, I've got the snow-making machine from the amusement park confirmed. They want to know where and when you want your snow." Ivy stood in the doorway.

Holly stared at her without answering.

"Holly?" Ivy entered the office uncertainly. "The snow? They asked if you have a permit. Shall I check on that for you?"

"Ivy..." Holly hesitated, then ran her fingers through her curls. "Ivy," she said again, "you remember the ballroom at the Landreth..."

"Uh-huh. About ten shades of red and orange. Clashes with everything."

"So you realize the problem."

Ivy looked at her with the first hint of suspicion. "Yes. That's why you're covering everything in white."

"I need at least three thousand dollars for a deposit on the silk," Holly said baldly.

"Wow. What does the ball committee say?"

Holly pretended to study the papers on her desk. "Nothing. I can't bother them with—"

"Then keep the room dark. The walls will look black that way. Too bad the carpet—"

"We could do it if we borrowed your college money," Holly interrupted quietly. "The ball committee can't reimburse me until afterward."

There was painful silence in the room.

Ivy's lower lip began to tremble. "I'm supposed to register next Tuesday."

"I'm sorry," Holly whispered. "I need the money for Mrs. Bloom, too. She's renting us the lights, the trees and the polar bears."

"What about all these people who are donating money and stuff?"

Holly winced at the bitterness in Ivy's voice. "It costs thousands of dollars to put on a ball like this. They hope to make hundreds of thousands."

Tears began to flow down Ivy's cheeks. "Can't you find a way to do it that doesn't cost so much?"

Holly felt horrible. "We decided to do this only if we made it spectacular. Otherwise, it won't do us any good."

"*You* decided."

Holly exhaled heavily. "Now I'm asking. If I could find another way to borrow the money, I would. Listen, after this, we'll be set for life. We'll never have to worry about money again. I promise you can enroll in the summer. You can go to any school you want. It's only four more months, Ivy."

Ivy wiped her cheeks and stood, clutching her papers. "I'll check on that permit for you."

"Ivy!"

Ivy, long black hair swirling around her, paused in the doorway with her back to Holly.

"You didn't say whether or not we could use your college money."

Ivy glanced back, her lips twisted in a bitter smile. "I understood my agreement was a mere formality. You're going to use it, anyway."

"Don't, Ivy."

"You want my blessing? Will that make you feel better? Or are you even capable of feeling guilty?"

Holly's stomach curled into a knot, as if she'd been punched. "If you tell me not to, I won't use your college money," she said evenly.

"Right," Ivy said, flinging up her arms, "so if anything goes wrong, it's my fault!"

"I'll be getting it back this time." Holly tried to smile. "In fact, why don't you check with the admissions department and see if there's a way to delay payment?"

"Don't treat me like a child, Holly. I'm not one anymore. You and I both know the college won't wait for payment, for the same reason no bank will lend you money. Bankruptcy and no tangible assets."

Holly sat at her desk for a few moments after Ivy left. Ivy was angry now, but she'd come around. She'd be grateful. Holly dialed the fabric mill. Ivy would go to the best school in the country. With a wardrobe to match. And a car.

And Holly would have a winter wonderland like no one had ever seen.

It was time to defrost the American Express card. Holly finished talking with the mills and had a rather tedious discussion with Mrs. Bloom. The concept of donating was foreign to her. They were arguing over whether she would supply a hundred white trees at cost, or at cost plus ten percent, when Holly noticed a shadow in the doorway.

"Mrs. Bloom, I'd like to stay on good terms with you, so I think I'll go with someone else." Holly hung up the phone with a feeling of great satisfaction. Let Bloomie call *her* for a change.

"So your telephone isn't out of order." The words were spoken with a deceptive mildness.

"Adam!" Holly exclaimed a little breathlessly. "What are you doing here?"

Adam walked over to her desk, leaned across it and tilted her chin with his fingers. "You haven't been sleeping," he said sternly. "You need this trip more than I thought."

Holly's face froze, then flushed with guilt. She tossed her head defensively.

Adam cleared a spot on her desk and spread out a travel brochure. "Warmth and sun, white beaches and our own cabana. Breakfast served on our private beach. No sight-seeing, no responsibilities, no worries."

Holly studied the brochure, feeling Adam's gaze on her bent head. He folded the leaflet and put it back in his breast pocket. "And no trip?"

"I . . ." Holly couldn't say anything else.

"I thought your phone was broken," he said conversationally. "I called. Several times. I haven't heard from you in three days."

Holly plastered a determined smile on her face. "The most incredible thing has happened. We're decorating for the Winter Ball. It's a chance I never thought we'd get. I happened to be in the right place at the right time."

Adam broke into her babble. "When is the Winter Ball, Holly?"

"The twenty-ninth."

"The day we're supposed to leave on our trip."

Holly felt uncomfortable with this quietly solemn Adam. He had the same look on his face that Laurel and Ivy had on theirs. He didn't understand. No one did. "I forgot."

"Forgot." The word hung between them.

"I'm sorry—I didn't mean that the way it sounded. Couldn't we postpone the trip? It sounds perfectly lovely and after this, I'll need it." Holly laughed shakily and ran her fingers through her hair. "Be happy for me. We'll get national coverage in the society pages. It'll be wonderful. You'll see."

There was no warmth in Adam's face. "Will I?"

"Yes." Holly looked at him in surprise. "You'll be there, won't you?"

"When were you planing to invite me?"

Holly threw down her pencil and sighed in exasperation. "I'm telling you about it now, okay?"

Adam strode around the side of her desk, withdrew the glossy leaflet with the ocean sunsets and private cabanas and thumbtacked it right in the middle of her scheduling board.

She had no warning. He grasped her shoulders and lifted her to her feet. He gazed at her an instant before crushing her slightly parted lips to his. Passion flared briefly within her before he set her roughly back in the chair. "Next time—ask."

CHAPTER NINE

HOLLY HALL WAS A WRECK, but a happy wreck. With her mother's diamonds glittering around her neck, Holly watched from her post near the ice-tunnel doorway as each group of people entered. Without fail, the newcomers gasped and exclaimed with delight as they left the twisting tunnel and entered a frosty world of enchantment.

Holly couldn't believe all the hard work was over and she had managed to pull it off. Fueled by caffeine, her brain had concocted a fantasy that had taken the carpenter and his crew a week of time-and-a-half to create.

The city of Dallas had graciously permitted artificial snow in front of the Landreth Hotel. Thousands of lights twinkled in white leafless tree branches as guests entered the hotel lobby. Outside the ballroom, they entered an igloolike tunnel with swirling fog, courtesy of a dry-ice machine. The tunnel twisted and turned before opening into a glittering white world.

Holly's only disappointment had been the silk. Who cared about its lovely draping qualities when the hideous color scheme of the ballroom showed through the thin fabric? Holly ended up shining colored lights on it like a theater scrim. She told everyone they were the northern lights.

"You know," Laurel remarked, noticing Holly studying the room, "it would have been less expensive to cover the walls with cheap dark fabric, hang lights and call them stars."

"Yes, it would have," Holly snapped. "That's a great idea. Why didn't you mention it?" How dared Laurel try to spoil her evening?

"You wouldn't have listened. You were determined to do it all by yourself." Laurel waved across the room. "There's Gus."

"That's not true! You had plenty of time to speak up!"

Laurel raised an eyebrow. "Really? Listen to yourself."

Holly brought a hand to her curls, jerking it back before she could succumb to her nervous habit. "We were all in this together."

Laurel adjusted the bodice of her silver lamé dress. "Whether we wanted to be or not."

She didn't expect gratitude, Holly told herself as she watched Laurel slink off. She took a deep breath, mentally composing herself and letting the feeling of triumph return.

This was her night. Holly Hall was back on top. She touched the necklace around her neck, knowing that it—or at least parts of it—was no stranger to opulent charity functions like this one. Amazingly, the few people she'd greeted didn't seem to remember the sordid accusations surrounding the financing of her father's last oil well. After dealing with the tedious legal processes for years, Holly felt everyone knew about the insurance company's claim that her father had deliberately set the well fire that had ultimately led to his death.

Dallas accepted her without question. Holly was light-headed with happiness as the last possible barrier to her success fell.

She beamed as she noticed Ivy approaching her through the crowd. Never mind Laurel. Ivy had come through for her. "Isn't this—" Holly hesitated "—perfect?"

The edge of Ivy's lips barely curved. "Here." She handed Holly a piece of paper.

Holly scanned it quickly. "He doesn't want to be paid right this minute, does he?" she asked tersely. How could the workmen present her with an invoice during the ball?

"It's a time card. The carpenters need you to sign it."

Holly frowned. "Hey, this is double time."

"You insisted that the men stay on call all night."

Holly scribbled her name on the sheet of paper. "Insurance. If anything collapses, help will be close by."

"Of course." Ivy took the paper from her and walked regally away, the daring white beaded dress she'd borrowed from Laurel earning her admiring looks.

So Ivy was angry at her, too. Great. Silver Siren and the Ice Princess. Sighing, Holly wandered over to the table where she'd left her coffee cup. Her polar bears, some recycled from Adam's tree for luck, cavorted on rock crystal.

Where was Adam, anyway? The crowd thickened. Restlessly Holly wandered around the perimeter of the ballroom, unnecessarily checking on the activities, her eyes darting to the tunnel entrance every few seconds.

A flash of light caught her eye, telling her Gus had begun photographing. Holly approached the sleigh set in front of a snowy backdrop. Gus had agreed to split half the profits of his souvenir photos with the Winter Ball committee. Mrs. Fitzhugh had accused Holly of a high-school prom mentality, but Holly had insisted on the photo gimmick. Couples posed in the sleigh, either as they were, or with the men borrowing a cape and top hat, and the women a fur-trimmed cloak.

Laurel, perched in the sleigh, leaned forward and crossed her legs, the clinging silver dress parting to reveal an inordinate amount of skin. Holly's eyes narrowed.

"Lighten up, Holly. They're supposed to be attracting attention." The Ice Princess had returned.

"And succeeding admirably." Holly smiled stiffly. "What are you eating?"

"Champagne ice from the Ice Palace." Ivy licked her spoon. "Do you think you might have overdone the ice theme a tad?"

"No!" Holly said sharply.

Ivy backed away. "Just asking."

Holly touched her sister's arm,. "Look . . . I didn't mean to snap at you. I just want everything to be perfect."

Reaching out, Ivy gently took Holly's coffee cup and set it on a table. "No more of this for you. Makes you jumpy."

"I can handle it."

Ivy shook her head. "Nope. You look like a hag as it is."

"I didn't spend all day getting ready, unlike some people." Holly darted an accusing glance toward Laurel, who had draped herself next to an older man she'd coaxed into posing with her.

"That's not fair!" Ivy lowered her voice. "Laurel traipsed all over town for you. Whose idea was the diamond ice, anyway? Who got the diamond gift certificates?"

Holly's shoulders sagged. "You're right. I'm sorry." Her buoyant spirit collapsed. "I don't know what's the matter with me."

Ivy's voice softened. "Too much caffeine. You'd be in worse shape, but Adam sent over some decaf beans and we've been mixing them in with your coffee."

"Adam did that?" Holly's spirits rose again.

"Yeah, remember him?" Ivy placed her empty glass next to Holly's coffee cup.

Holly exhaled forcefully. "Adam knew how it was going to be. I didn't make him any promises."

Ivy fingered the white silk of Holly's dress. "It wouldn't have mattered if you had, would it?"

A numbing pain started in Holly's chest and radiated outward. Ivy met her look without apology. There was a bitterness in Ivy's eyes that recalled the day they'd quarreled about the money.

Holly took a deep breath as the pain lessened. "Things don't always happen the way we'd like them to."

Ivy's gaze shifted to just over Holly's shoulder. Holly turned and saw Adam striding toward them.

He'd come! With the way her sisters had been acting, Holly had half expected not to see Adam tonight. But here he was, coming to share her success.

It was the first time she had seen or spoken to him since he'd walked out of her office that day. Holly felt a rush of pride as she watched his approach. His tuxedo fit perfectly and was an elegant, unadorned black. The errant lock of hair, which usually fell onto his forehead, had been tamed. He looked wonderful. She'd missed him so much. Maybe they could take that trip together next weekend. . . .

"Adam!" Holly laughingly threw herself at his chest.

Knocked off balance by Holly's unexpected greeting, Adam held her close, steadying her before gently unwrapping her arms.

"I knew you'd come!" Happiness shone in her eyes.

"Did you?" Adam asked quietly, his blue eyes cold.

Holly's smile froze. Not Adam, too. Everyone who meant anything to her had abandoned her during this project. Hadn't she learned she could depend only on herself?

"Ivy." Adam's gaze warmed as he greeted her sister. "You look stunning." His eyes flicked over Holly. "You look horrible."

"Thanks a lot."

"White isn't your color."

"Black isn't either, anymore," Ivy commented. "She ran herself down so much, her dress didn't fit, so we sewed her a new one out of the leftover silk."

"Figures." Adam's face softened slightly as he saw beneath Holly's indomitable facade. "When was the last time you ate?"

Without waiting for an answer, he propelled Holly toward the kitchen. "Are those mascara smudges or circles under your eyes?"

"Why did you bother to come?" Holly jerked her arm away. "You're spoiling everything. Leave me alone."

Adam ignored her. "Sit." He pushed her into a seat among the white branches ringing the room and started to go through the doors into the kitchen.

"Hey, don't bother the caterers," Holly called after him even as the scent of food wafted through the open door.

Adam gave her a disgusted look and disappeared through the doors. He returned in moments, bearing a plate of food. "Eat."

Holly clenched her jaw mutinously.

Adam set the plate on her lap. "Eat, or I'll force-feed you, creating precisely the kind of scene you wish to avoid tonight."

The shrimp looked delicious. Suddenly ravenous, Holly tried one. She reached for the glass Adam patiently held for her, drank and grimaced. "This isn't champagne."

"Apple juice."

Adam sat back on the silk-covered folding chair and watched Holly devour the food. Had she been trying to kill herself?

Adam's fury had faded the moment he'd seen Holly. Her eyes were enormous in a sallow haggard face. Even her curls had lost their bounce. He wondered if she'd thought about him at all during the past two weeks. He wondered if she'd guessed he had decided not to see her again.

It was too painful to dream about what they might have had together. His lips tightened. Too painful for him. Holly didn't appear to be affected one way or the other. But she needed him, couldn't she see that?

Just as he needed her.

"Ivy was right." Holly stared at her empty plate. "I've been drinking too much coffee."

One corner of Adam's mouth lifted just enough to hint at a dimple.

"I'm glad you're here." Holly leaned her head against Adam's shoulder, causing him to sigh with resignation. "What's the matter?"

"I'm glad I'm here too."

Holly nestled closer and Adam curled his arm around her. A passing waiter took her plate and they sat for several minutes listening to the soft music from the harps and watching people discover the grottoes and explore the Ice Palace.

"This is beautiful, Holly. I hope it brings you every success." Adam waited for an acknowledgment and some comment on her future plans.

The harpists finished their piece on a rippling chord. As they changed their music, Adam heard Holly's slow even breathing. She was asleep.

Chuckling to himself, Adam retrieved her purse from the floor, turned her in his arms, picked her up and carried her out the door to the corridor outside the kitchen. Swiftly ducking into a meeting room, Adam gently set Holly on a mound of leftover silk and closed the door.

He shrugged out of his tuxedo jacket and laid it over her. With luck, she could sleep undisturbed for a few minutes. All the extra chairs, tablecloths and crockery were stored in here. With hors d'oeuvres just now being served, this stuff shouldn't be needed for about half an hour.

Adam watched Holly sleep. She was noticeably thinner and must have been completely exhausted to collapse during her big evening. He shook his head, smiling wryly. He didn't dare let her sleep through the whole thing.

The unflattering fluorescent light and stark white material leeched color from Holly's already pallid skin. She still looked beautiful to Adam. Beautiful and independent. Strong and stubborn.

He'd noticed his polar bears, too, and strongly suspected that was Bianca, the polar-bear rug, making another appearance, this time on a Styrofoam ice floe.

So Holly felt something for him, right? But was it enough?

The harp music had stopped and Adam listened to the sounds from the ballroom. Within moments, a string quartet began playing, the music muted by the walls.

Adam reached out and ran a finger over Holly's cheek. There were men who would be noble in situations like this. He didn't plan to be one of them.

Time for Sleeping Beauty to awaken. Adam bent over her and kissed her lightly. No response. At least she hadn't bolted upright and crashed into his head.

He settled next to her, gathering her into his arms. For several minutes he was content just to hold her, savoring their first peaceful moment alone in almost a month.

They should have been on a beach tonight, their bodies caressed by warm sea breezes and pillowed by sand. Adam closed his eyes for a moment, almost able to smell the salty tang of the ocean.

Eyes still closed, he began a gentle trail of kisses from Holly's temple down the side of her neck, where her pulse beat slowly and steadily.

Holly was zonked.

Sighing heavily, Adam jiggled her slightly. "Holly?"

Someone shattered her lovely dream. "Go away."

Adam tugged at his jacket. "If I did that, you'd never forgive me."

"I will, I promise." Holly drifted back onto her cloud and waited for the lovely sensations to begin again. But now the cloud was cold and wet.

"Hey!" She wiped her forehead. It hadn't been raining in her dream.

Holly opened her eyes. Adam stood over her tilting a pitcher of ice water.

"Stop, you'll ruin the silk." Holly struggled to sit up.

Adam knelt and gently wiped her face with some of the napkins piled in the room.

"Did I fall asleep?" Holly took a napkin from Adam and finished drying off.

"Yes," Adam affirmed, smiling affectionately. "Feel better?"

"Kind of groggy." She looked at him in alarm. "How long did I sleep?"

"Twenty minutes or so." Adam sat next to her. "Don't worry, I wouldn't let you miss your big night."

"Oh, Adam." Holly's shoulders sagged. "Why do you put up with me?"

He gazed at her steadily before clasping her shoulders and drawing her toward him. "Because, Holly, I love you."

"You do?" She looked up and found the love radiating from his eyes. "I thought you were mad at me."

"I was—am." He gave her a rueful smile. "But as I discovered in the last two weeks, it is very possible to love someone and feel like strangling her at the same time."

"I always feel that way about my sisters."

"I do *not* think of you as my sister!"

Holly smiled and settled back onto the silk. "Prove it."

A split second later, Adam covered her mouth with his. If she thought she could say something like that and get away with it just because they were in a not-so-private room surrounded by hundreds of people, any one of whom could, and probably would, burst in on them...well, Ms. Hall was about to learn a thing or two about men who had been deprived of their weekend in the sun.

Adam kissed her for all the days he'd spent working himself into a stupor at the law firm, trying to forget her. Then he kissed her for the days they'd been apart, the hours of their lost weekend and the exasperating trouble Holly had been. Then he kissed her for the heck of it.

In the back of his mind, Adam was aware that unleashing the emotional torrent raging inside him was not a good idea. He began to pull back before his voice of reason drowned completely.

Holly's already had. The rising tide of passion swept her away. As Adam pulled back, Holly moved forward, nudging him backward until he was enveloped in masses of white silk.

He could stay like this forever, Adam thought, breathing in the unique scent Holly wore. The string quartet's music serenaded them, changing from fast-paced Vivaldi to a slower lusher sound.

Their kisses changed, too, from frantic caresses to deeply sensual ones.

Adam buried his face in the side of Holly's neck, his hands stroking the shoulders left bare by the cut of her dress. He wanted her so much he ached. Wrapping his arms around her in a tight embrace he tried to calm his breathing.

"Ouch."

Adam released her instantly. "Did I hurt you?" he managed to ask, his voice hoarse.

Holly propped herself on her elbows above him. "Mama's necklace," she gasped, looking down at her neck.

Adam's gaze followed hers, fastening on the deep red marks made by the stones as they pressed into her soft flesh.

"I'm sorry," he whispered, raising his head and gently kissing the worst of the marks.

Holly sighed and rolled away from him. "It's just as well, don't you think?" She smiled sheepishly.

"Ask me again in a few minutes." Adam lay on the silk, his eyes closed.

Holly got to her feet, ineffectively brushing at the wrinkles in her dress. In a few minutes, Adam stood beside her, shrugging on his coat.

"I told you once that I loved you, but you didn't believe me." Holly tried to keep the hurt out of her voice.

Adam gave her a wicked grin. "I know exactly which parts of you love me. I'm holding out for all of you."

Puzzled, Holly watched him straighten his tie and cummerbund. "What do you mean?"

"How many brothers and sisters do I have?"

Holly blinked.

"What's my favorite food? Where's my home?"

"Boston," Holly answered quickly.

"That's where my family lives—do I live there? What's my address?"

"I don't have it. You live in Dallas now."

Adam nodded. "I'll concede that. What are my favorite sports? Where did I go to school? What's my favorite color?"

"Blue," Holly guessed, desperately.

A smile lit Adam's face, making her feel worse. "How did you know?"

"All men like blue," she mumbled.

Adam sighed. "What are my plans for the future?"

Holly glared at him. "All right, you made your point."

"Did I?" he asked, quietly.

"I'm free all day tomorrow. Want to find out?" Holly held out her hand and Adam took it, lacing his fingers through hers.

They stood, smiling at each other, until the rumble of dish-laden carts reminded them where they were.

"Dinner," they both said at the same time and laughed. Adam opened the door, beckoned to her and they escaped down the hall away from the kitchen.

"Where have you been?" Laurel whispered when Adam and Holly slipped into their places at the table reserved for them.

"Checking on this and that. You know Holly." Adam's smile included everyone around him—especially Laurel.

"Welcome, friends and patrons of the arts." Mrs. Fitzhugh began to speak from the head table. Laurel narrowed her eyes suspiciously at Holly before turning to listen.

Mrs. Fitzhugh informed them that this Winter Ball was the most successful ever. "And I understand that as of this moment, several diamonds have not yet been discovered. Waiters will be circulating with bags of ice. Ten dollars might buy you quite a rock. Be assured, the diamond you find may be exchanged for the real thing."

"Whose idea was that?" Adam asked.

"Honey," drawled the voice on his left, "don't you know that diamonds are a girl's best friend?" Laurel gave him an outrageous wink.

Mrs. Fitzhugh continued, "Among the many who made this evening possible, none worked harder than Holly Hall of Deck the Halls, who stepped in at the last minute to create this winter wonderland. Thank you, Holly!"

The applause was thunderous. Holly rose to acknowledge it, grasping Adam's hand tightly. Instead of quieting, the noise swelled in a crescendo as the ball committee stood, followed by everyone at the tables.

As she soaked in the sweet sound of the applause, Holly knew she would never forget this moment. It had taken more than five years of scrambling to reach the top and now she intended to stay there.

Adam tightened the pressure on her hand so much that she glanced at him in surprise. He nodded slightly toward her sisters.

Belatedly, Holly gestured toward them and applauded. Ivy, wearing a tight smile, inclined her head. Laurel threw kisses to the crowd.

Holly floated through the rest of the evening. She sparkled, she bubbled and she worked the crowd like a pro. Throughout the night, Adam was at her side. She held his hand or his arm, her eyes seeking his every few minutes.

At last, it was over.

"Holly, you saved the ball for us. We won't forget it."

Holly smiled at the venerable society matron. "Just think of Deck the Halls the next time you entertain."

"I will, dear. Martha's and Claudia's tedious rivalry has done some good, after all."

As the hotel workers moved in to clear the room, Holly and Adam stood arm in arm. "It *is* great, isn't it?"

Adam laughed. "Haven't you had enough compliments for one evening?"

"Never. I hate to undo all that work, but I'm paying a crew double and it's time they earned it." She looked at Adam. "I'm going to change into some jeans and pack up the rented stuff. Want to stay and help?"

Laurel and Ivy had already changed and begun dragging boxes into the room. "Hey, Cinderella, it struck midnight," Laurel said.

"More like 1 a.m." Adam removed his jacket and tie.

"Holly, it looks like a bunch of Mrs. Bloom's bears have disappeared." Ivy had a worried frown on her face.

"Yeah, pretty light-fingered for a well-heeled crowd." Laurel stood, hands on her hips, and surveyed the room. "I'm going to check in the kitchen and make sure the caterers know not to throw anything away until we look through it first. Maybe I'll find some of the bears in the trash."

"Not to mention leftovers," Holly murmured to Adam. "Ivy, keep a count of the missing bears and I'll add it to my expense sheet."

"What about all these trees and lights?" Adam asked.

"The work crew will dismantle those. Why don't you get Bianca? I think we used a hanging bag to transport her."

Holly grabbed her jeans and headed for the restroom.

"Holly!" Mrs. Fitzhugh and her committee were adding up receipts from the diamond ice and Gus's photography. "We're just getting a preliminary tally, but the ball has been a tremendous success."

"Oh." Holly set her jeans on a table and dug in her purse. "You'll want this then." She handed Mrs. Fitzhugh an envelope. "It's just an estimate right now, but it will help you figure your profit."

"Goodness." Mrs. Fitzhugh glanced at the long list and initialed it. "We'll send you a formal letter for tax purposes, of course," she said, handing the paper back to Holly.

"Don't you need these numbers? I have to warn you, some of the table decorations seem to have walked off and the rental company will have to be paid for those."

Mrs. Fitzhugh nodded absently and went back to tallying the cash.

"Mrs. Fitzhugh? It's very late, so I'll leave this with you to look over and we can discuss the expenses tomorrow or Monday. I have some statements here." Holly reached into the envelope and handed them to Mrs. Fitzhugh.

"What are these?" Mrs. Fitzhugh looked at Holly blankly.

Maybe she was tired. Holly certainly was. "These are invoices from the rental company, some fabric mills, the amusement park for the snow-making machine out front and the work crews, who are dismantling the sets." Holly waved a hand around the room. Adam was a few feet away and came to stand beside her.

"They're your responsibility, Holly." Mrs. Fitzhugh handed her back the invoices. "I thought you understood."

"You'd rather I pay them and you'll reimburse me." Holly nodded, wondering how she'd manage that. She'd just have to figure everything up and submit her bill pronto.

But Mrs. Fitzhugh shook her head. "There is no question of reimbursement. You agreed to donate your services."

"And I did. These are my out-of-pocket expenses. I didn't charge you for my time." Holly's eyes flicked to the piles of cash the women were counting. Cash they wouldn't have if she and Laurel hadn't come up with the photos, the diamond ice and the wishing pond in the Ice Palace.

"I should hope not. We're a charity organization, dear. We raise money. Everything is donated, otherwise we wouldn't have such successful fund-raisers."

"It is understood that all fund-raising events generate expenses, Mrs. Fitzhugh," Adam said in his lawyer voice, and Holly laid a warning hand on his arm.

"*Reasonable* expenses."

"I had less than three weeks, Mrs. Fitzhugh." This couldn't be happening! "If more time had been available, I might have found companies willing to donate materials and labor." Holly swallowed as five stony society faces glared at her. "Under the circumstances, you should expect some extra expense this year."

"We certainly didn't give you carte blanche to spend all the profits!" Mrs. Fitzhugh's hoarse voice began to carry.

Holly's temper rose, along with her panic. "If I hadn't stepped in, you wouldn't have had a ball!"

"While we are certainly grateful, you must understand how it is if you want to continue to work at this level of so-

ciety. You gain the exposure and write your expenses off to
advertising or charity or something. We've never had to pay
for anything but the room and a minimal amount for food.''
Mrs. Fitzhugh shook her head. ''I was afraid of this when I
agreed to work with an amateur.''

A cold feeling settled in the pit of Holly's stomach. ''I am
a professional.''

''Mr. Kelly would have understood.'' The others murmured and nodded.

''Mr. Kelly backed out,'' Adam inserted, but Holly
gripped his arm.

''I apologize for the misunderstanding, Mrs. Fitzhugh.''
Holly's tight smile included the crones seated around her.
''And I look forward to working with you all in the fu-
ture.''

CHAPTER TEN

"Don't be a fool, Holly!" Adam paced in front of the wing chair where Holly sat, tightly curled up. He'd been saying the same thing, or a variation of it, all night long.

"Stop badgering me." The dull resignation in Holly's voice alarmed Adam more than if she'd snapped at him.

"Let me help you. Legally, you're in a strong position to—"

"No."

Adam rubbed the back of his neck as he glared at Holly. Impossible woman. Sighing audibly, he paced to the front window and drew back the curtains. A pinkish-gray dawn greeted him. "How much did you spend?" he asked, without turning around.

"Everything."

The breath hissed between his teeth as Adam let the curtains fall back into place. "Look." He crossed the room swiftly and knelt in front of her. "You're playing right into Mrs. Fitzhugh's hands." His lips tightened. "These women all compete with each other. She wants this ball to raise the most money, and anything she has to spend takes away from the profits."

Holly turned her eyes to him. His once immaculately crisp shirt was a network of wrinkles. She reached out a finger and ran it over his stubble-shaded jaw. "That's a sexy look for you."

"Holly." Adam pulled her hand away and held it between both of his. "Mrs. Fitzhugh is treating you as a social equal."

"And I'm just the hired help?"

Adam spoke very gently. "In essence, yes. She wouldn't have tried this with anyone else."

"I'll make it back." The fire was missing from her voice.

"How many jobs is it going to take before you do? Wait a couple of hours and call the Fitzhugh woman and insist that she reimburse you." Adam could see Holly had no intention of following his advice. "Better yet, I'll do it—as your lawyer."

"No." Holly tugged her hand away. "If I do that, no one will ever hire me again. I'll be blackballed."

"Hardly. You're a terrific bargain." Adam got to his feet and looked down at her. "You're supposed to be running a business. Now act like it. That is, assuming you have a business left."

Holly huddled in the chair. "I built it once. I can do it again."

Adam wanted to shake her. "Listen to yourself! You're allowing them to wipe out five years of work."

"I won't be starting over completely. I have the Christmas stock and I have *contacts*." The word was a talisman.

"That Fitzhugh woman has some kind of gall. You saved her neck." Adam shoved his hands in his pockets—another gesture he'd been repeating for hours. "I suppose it's pointless to ask if you had a contract?"

Her eyes briefly met his.

"Great." Adam jiggled the change in his pockets for a minute. "Did you ever discuss a budget?"

Holly shifted her legs. "No. I kept her informed of my plans, but she never questioned anything I spent."

Adam stared at her in disbelief. "That's no way to run a charity ball. Then again, it was brilliant. Poor Holly. Don't you understand? She set you up right from the start."

"Actually, I got the idea she was so happy just to *have* a ball that anything I spent was all right."

"Unbelievable." Adam began to pace again. "What are you going to tell Ivy and Laurel?"

Holly's laugh was mirthless. "Big sister miscalculated."

"Let's see by how much." Adam glanced around the living room, before sitting down at her mother's writing desk. "When you said you spent everything, did you mean a lot or . . . everything?"

Holly gave a crack of laughter. "I spent it all and then some. I have bills coming in and I defrosted the charge card."

Adam didn't laugh. "Get your receipts and any outstanding bills. I assume you kept records."

With a contemptuous look, Holly unfolded herself from the chair. "Start on this," she said, handing Adam her notebook.

Adam was working on that when Holly returned and dumped the contents of a file folder, a calculator and a frosty foil-wrapped package on the desk, then returned to the chair.

"What's this?" Adam held up the frozen package.

"I overlooked that one. We found it last night when we put all that food in the freezer. It's money."

Adam's dimples appeared. "Your total, uh, liquid assets?"

Holly nodded, watching as Adam studied the receipts and bills. She supposed she should feel really horrible, but she didn't. She'd make all the money back, and it wouldn't take her five years, either. This was an expensive lesson and one she didn't intend to repeat.

"Okay." Adam stared at the figures. "Here's what we're going to do."

"Oh, really?"

"Be quiet. We're transferring some of your expenses. Today, you're going to have a chat with the hotel conference manager. The dishes and the tables—where did you get those?"

For the first time, there was a brief flicker of interest in Holly's eyes. "From the hotel."

Adam held up a piece of paper. "This is a bill for white dishes. There isn't anything unusual about white dishes—why did they charge you for them?"

"The hotel's had colored bands. I asked for plain white."

Adam smiled. "Fine. But supplying dishes is the hotel's problem or the caterer's problem—not your problem. You're going to instruct them to add that to their bill to the Winter Ball committee." He put it aside. "See how painless that was?"

"But—"

"Tables and chairs?"

Holly began to smile. "The hotel."

Adam added to the small stack. "Labor?"

"I used a set designer from a theater group."

"Did he hire the workers?"

Holly sat up. "No, the hotel got them for me."

"Then let them bill the hotel. Claudia Fitzhugh isn't about to tangle with the Landreth."

Holly slipped out of her chair and came across the room to stand beside Adam. "How does it look?"

Adam turned the sheet he'd been writing on toward her. "That takes care of half your expenses right there."

"Thank you, Adam." Holly bent down and wrapped her arms around him.

The phone rang. Holly jerked. "You see? It's started. I'll pull out of this."

She ran to answer the phone, waving a piece of paper triumphantly when she returned. "A Valentine luncheon— what did I tell you?"

"Is it for charity?" Adam asked cynically.

Holy shook her head. The phone rang again.

"Don't these people go to church?" Adam grumbled.

Holly skipped back. "I'm getting booked for all the holidays. Fourth of July at the country club."

"Have them sign a contract, which I'll draw up. Then call Mrs. Fitzhugh, apologize for not making it clear that you were donating your services in a professional capacity, and offer to split your expenses."

"Adam . . ." Holly began, a warning in her voice.

"That's called compromise, my dear. My specialty. Everybody walks away with something."

The phone rang a third time. And a fourth.

"I'm going home," Adam announced, when it became apparent that he wouldn't get any more uninterrupted conversation with Holly. "I'll draft a standard contract for you so you won't be in a mess like this again.

"What mess?" A rumpled Laurel put in her first appearance of the morning.

"That's my exit cue." Adam kissed Holly on the cheek. "Hang in there," he whispered and let himself out the front door.

Her sisters handled the news the way Holly had expected they would. Laurel screamed and Ivy cried.

"I don't care what Mrs. Fitzhugh and those other biddies think," Ivy declared. "We should go and demand our money. My *college* money."

Laurel nodded. "You always said we were in this together. Well, I'm with Ivy. You can't decide all by yourself to write it off." They'd moved to the kitchen and Laurel poured them each another cup of coffee. Ivy wrinkled her nose and diluted hers with three sugars and a generous slug of milk.

"Look at this." Holly picked up the notes she'd made from the morning's phone calls. "We're booked for most major holidays for the rest of this year. If I raise a stink, they'll cancel."

Laurel stared at her a moment. "That might not be so bad."

Holly's protest was cut off by the telephone. Laurel stood up quickly to answer it.

Holly took another sip of coffee, careful not to gulp it down, as she observed Ivy's stormy face. "I know what I said about your going to college and I'm sure that by September, you can."

"Really?" Ivy gave Holly a disgusted look and went to raid the refrigerator. It was packed with last night's leftovers, which Laurel had sweet-talked out of the caterers. "Work on the Christmas trees now and go to college later. Look where that got me."

"Gripe, gripe, gripe. Adam says to check the society section and call Mrs. Fitzhugh this afternoon. She'll be mellower then," Laurel said, hanging up the phone.

Ivy emptied a bag of once-elegant, slightly wilted party food as Holly dug out the Sunday newspaper society section.

Laurel spread the paper on the table. The center two pages were devoted to candid photographs of the Winter Ball.

"You see!" Holly stabbed the paper triumphantly. "There are as many pictures of the decor as there are of the personalities. That's why I can't sabotage this kind of exposure by whining about the money to Mrs. Fitzhugh."

"Whining!" Ivy protested. "We're talking about thousands!"

Her sisters were impossible. "That's what we're talking about if I lose these new jobs."

"Hey, here I am. Laurel Hall, Our Town's aspiring actress—"

"Actress?" Holly leaned over the paper and scanned the text. "You were interviewed and didn't mention Deck the Halls?"

Laurel looked surprised. "Admit I was the hired help?"

"Would have solved a few problems," Holly said dryly.

"There are three pictures of Laurel posing with those old men in the sleigh." Ivy pointed to them.

"Oh, no," Holly groaned. "She looks like she's about to fall out of that dress."

"Oh, piffle," Laurel said. "Those men were sweet. Their wives are on the committee."

Holly winced. "I'll bet they just love this." She sighed. "I'd better get to Mrs. Fitzhugh before they do."

As Adam had predicted, Mrs. Fitzhugh was all smiles, until she saw her caller was Holly.

"Enjoying your success?" Holly asked as she led the way into Mrs. Fitzhugh's study.

"I was." The unblinking matron declined to sit, forcing Holly to stand, too.

Holly handed her a brown envelope. "This is a revised list of the ball's expenses." When Mrs. Fitzhugh made no move to take it, Holly carefully placed the envelope on the cherrywood desk. "I apologize for not making it clearer that you were dealing with me in a professional capacity." The words nearly stuck in her throat.

"I find that, in your inexperience, you have been wildly extravagant. The Winter Ball committee authorized none of the expenses.'' Mrs. Fitzhugh's smile was a mixture of triumph, pity and smugness.

"I hoped we'd be able to reach a compromise," Holly stated, looking into a watery blue gaze that was the twin of Mr. Steele's.

"It will cost you more than it's worth." The threat was implicit in each well-modulated word.

Holly walked out of the study. "I'll have all further invoices directed to the Winter Ball committee."

"Do that and you won't work in Dallas again."

"I BELIEVE YOU'VE MET my sister, Claudia Fitzhugh."

Adam smiled and nodded, taking in the rigid posture of Mrs. Fitzhugh and the rest of the Winter Ball committee, stiffly perched on the leather furniture in Mr. Steele's plush office. No one returned his smile.

"Have you seen this?" Mr. Steele whirled around and thrust something at Adam, obviously hoping to catch him off guard.

"A pinup calendar?" Grimacing with distaste, Adam shook his head and tossed the calendar back on the desk. "Not my style."

Mr. Steele retrieved it, flipped through the pages and turned it around to face Adam. "Care to comment?"

It was the penthouse with the skyline view, Bianca, the fireplace tools and, unfortunately, Darlene, the receptionist.

Mrs. Fitzhugh sniffed. "It appears Bernard has a penchant for hiring floozies."

"Claudia," Mr. Steele warned as he awaited Adam's reaction.

Adam, drawing on years of lawyer-family upbringing, kept his face carefully neutral. "I know nothing about it."

"Kinda thing you find in army barracks—or service stations," Mr. Steele said. "In fact, one of our clients found this in a service station. One of his. Wanted to know why he got a picture of a tree and his employees got her." Mr. Steele laughed, but Adam wasn't deceived. "We look like fools."

"Darlene is an excellent receptionist. This shouldn't—"

Mr. Steele waved away Adam's comment. "I don't blame her—it was that Hall gal. Brilliant. I underestimated her. She's still mad 'cause I wouldn't represent her after the crash. Purely a business decision, but she was too green to see it that way. Stood right where you are now and told me she'd never forget it. That I'd regret my... betrayal, I think she called it." Mr. Steele smiled in remembrance.

"Are you implying that this is her revenge?" Adam forced amusement into his voice.

"Superbly planned, too." Mr. Steele thrust out his lower lip and stared at his shoes. "Too bad she's not a lawyer."

Claudia Fitzhugh could remain silent no longer. "My ball, Bernard! That girl and her strumpet of a sister used me and embarrassed the committee. And your new partner's involvement in this entire—" She stopped abruptly as she noted the anger in Adam's eyes.

"Be very sure of yourself before you make accusations." Adam's words were chiseled, his face like stone.

"It's obvious to anyone!" Mrs. Fitzhugh thrust the Sunday society section at Adam and pointed a jeweled finger at the pages of color photographs of the ball. "Look how she insinuated her sister into these pictures. Look at that dress!"

Adam found it difficult to control his mounting fury. "You should complain to the newspaper. They chose the pictures."

"It says she is an *actress*." Mrs. Fitzhugh said the word in a tone that indicated she felt it was synonymous with call girl. "The ballet is hardly mentioned."

There was a whispered comment from the committee. Mrs. Fitzhugh nodded her head. "Do you know how many of the men were forced to pose in the sleigh with her instead of their wives?"

Adam's gaze flicked over some of those wives. "No," he said blandly. "But it was for charity, wasn't it?"

"Tainted money," Mrs. Fitzhugh declared. "And speaking of money—" she imperiously held out a hand and an envelope magically appeared in it "—this . . . this is a demand for payment. Not only did Ms. Hall use our ball to further her sister's career, she actually wants the committee to pay for it!"

Adam took the envelope from Mrs. Fitzhugh and glanced at the papers inside. Holly hadn't varied from the figures he'd calculated. He nodded and handed the papers to Mr. Steele. "Everything appears to be in order."

"How can you say that?" Mrs. Fitzhugh quivered indignantly. "She was outrageously extravagant!"

"Just on the silk, but she's offering to split expenses down the middle there. You must admit, the room was spectacular."

More whispering from the committee. "Nevertheless, she must pay for her exorbitance. We'll sue her if she refuses."

"Claudia," began Mr. Steele heavily.

"Stop waffling, Bernard. Are you with us or this poor besotted young man?"

The challenge hung in the air. Mr. Steele's faded blue eyes traveled from his sister and her friends, whose husbands represented some of his largest corporate accounts, to Adam.

"Ladies." Adam turned to the disapproving women, making an effort to sound conciliatory without being patronizing. "Let's meet in a couple of days when tempers have cooled." He smiled the devastating smile that could turn Holly's bones to water. "I'm sure you want to avoid dragging this into the public eye."

"It's already public." Mrs. Fitzhugh abruptly changed targets. "Mr. Markland, since you are living in the penthouse, tell us when *this*—" she walked to the desk and picked up the calendar, holding it as if it threatened to contaminate her "—was photographed."

Barely controlled fury radiated from Adam. "I have said I know nothing of it." His voice rang with the authority of two generations of Markland lawyers. "I will remind you that I am unaccustomed to having my word questioned."

"I believe you, Adam." Mr. Steele's attempt at conciliation failed with his next words. "But not everyone does. It looks to me like we'll have to take this case. I'm still going to let you handle it though." Mr. Steele's jowls stretched into a smile as if he had handed Adam a gift.

Adam turned his piercing gaze on him. "I'm no longer a trial lawyer." The brilliant blue eyes shaded by thick black brows were an intimidating Markland weapon. Adam used them now. "This can be settled out of court."

Mr. Steele backed off, as others had before him. "You're right, Adam."

"Are you refusing?" trilled Mrs. Fitzhugh, with a furious look at her brother. "It appears you have something to hide, Bernard. A penthouse tryst with your receptionist, perhaps?"

Adam watched Mr. Steele's face turn a dull redbrick color. Mrs. Fitzhugh, bolstered by her committee, was in fine form. When he recovered, Adam knew Bernard Steele would bend to the wishes of his sister.

"I've heard enough." Adam's voice sliced through the heavy silence. "I want it understood that before you accept this case, I am resigning my partnership in Swinehart, Cathardy and Steele. You'll have a letter within fifteen minutes.''

"Adam!" It was the first time Mr. Steele had raised his voice. "You're thinking below the waist."

Adam lifted an eyebrow and turned to leave, quietly closing the door. He stood for a moment, his eyes tightly shut. Holly. He had to go to her.

HOLLY SAW ADAM'S CAR from her bedroom window.

"Hi," he said softly, when she answered the door.

He stood looking at her, but not really seeing her. Holly noted the lines of strain around his mouth and the bleakness in his eyes. Wordlessly, she opened her arms and he came to her, hugging her fiercely.

"Let's go sit down." Holly began to rub his neck and back.

Adam relaxed. "Feels good." He smiled wearily at her and drew a gentle finger along her cheek.

Holly turned her face into his palm and kissed it.

Words began to pour out of Adam as Holly listened silently. He told her about his lawyer family and the challenge of growing up a Markland. He liked law, he said, but wasn't a fanatic about it. He refused to separate the law from people and preferred arbitration over going to trial. His family had been subtle and then overt in their disapproval.

Holly listened, conscious that she was learning more about Adam now than in the months she'd known him. As he talked, she began to understand what he'd meant about her not being *in* love with him. Quite suddenly, she realized she wanted to spend all the evenings for the rest of her life listening to Adam discuss his work and his feelings, and sharing hers with him. Adam was right—there was a difference.

"What happened today?" Holly asked softly. For once, she forgot about Deck the Halls. There was only Adam and right now he needed her.

Adam released a lungful of air and closed his eyes. "I resigned my partnership today."

"Why?"

He hesitated. "They're about to take a high-profile case that has no business in court. I'm trying to prevent it. They wanted me to handle it."

"Couldn't you win it?" Holly asked, trying to understand.

"Yes." He opened his eyes, but didn't look at her. "I could win it."

"Then why not accept it? Adam, you've spent hours negotiating behind the scenes. This would put you in the spotlight." Holly unconsciously began a pep talk like the ones she'd given her sisters hundreds of times.

"I'm not a trial lawyer." A touch of irritation entered his voice.

"But you said you could win it."

Adam turned toward her. "Winning isn't everything, trite as that sounds. People would get hurt. It might destroy a family business."

"So? Someone has to lose. Is this another bankruptcy case?"

"It's headed that way."

Holly didn't like feeling disloyal to Adam, but she owed him her opinion. "People and businesses go bankrupt all the time. It happens. It happened to us and nobody was worried about where we'd get our next meal."

Adam opened his mouth, then closed it abruptly, obviously changing his mind. "There's a little more to it than I've told you," he commented at last.

"I still think you should take it. If you don't, another lawyer will and get all the publicity."

"Holly— I resigned," Adam said, biting off each word.

Holly was trying so hard to encourage Adam to grab the opportunity, she missed the warning tone in his voice.

"Don't you have any ambition?" Holly asked, filling her voice with amazement. Maybe he'd try to prove her wrong.

Adam got to his feet. "I have principles and I refuse to sacrifice them on the altar of money."

"Glad you can afford them," Holly said dryly. "Not everyone can."

Adam stared at her, his face drained of color. "It was a mistake to come here." He started for the door.

"I don't believe this!" Holly shouted, running after him. "You're leaving just because I disagreed with your decision?"

Adam paused at the door. "I . . . wanted your support."

Holly gripped his arms. "I'm not ever going to agree with you when I think you're wrong."

"I thought you'd understand. You've made decisions everybody thought were wrong, but you believed in yourself. This time, I expected you to trust my judgment," Adam said quietly.

"Even when it's wrong?"

The bleakness returned to Adam's eyes. His gaze roamed over her features, as if committing them to memory. He leaned down and kissed her on the forehead. "Goodbye."

His goodbye made her very nervous, even though Holly told herself she was right to give Adam her honest opinion. He was just stewing over it for a while, but she was confident he'd come around. He ought to know she wasn't some fluff-brained creature who would agree with anything he said or did.

Guilt, her favorite emotion, settled in the next day. Mrs. Fitzhugh refused to take her calls, but the hotel and caterers agreed to bill the committee directly. Mrs. Bloom howled about losses and damages. Holly wearily promised to pay for the bears, but not for normal wear and tear on the white trees.

"Holly? Lunch." Laurel popped into and out of Holly's office.

At least there were no surprises there—party leftovers.

"How's the money situation?" Laurel asked.

"I can't get through to Mrs. Fitzhugh, so I don't know if our suppliers are getting paid or not. We have one month's expenses in the freezer, but we've got credit-card balances." Holly smiled with false brightness. "Fortunately, I already paid our taxes on the house, or we'd be out that, too. Thank heaven Ivy went back to Exemp Temps. I'm still working on Bloomie."

"And the silk?"

Holly shook her head. "One mill offered about ten cents on the dollar to take it back—"

Ivy burst into the kitchen, clutching papers. "Holly, we're being sued!" She thrust the papers at Holly and sat at the kitchen table trying to catch her breath.

"What is this?" Holly tried to make sense of the papers.

"Exemplary Temporaries sent me to a law firm and I've been typing. This was in the stack."

"Are you at Swinehart, Cathardy and Steele?" Holly began to feel sick.

Ivy nodded.

"That's Adam's firm," Laurel whispered.

"Was," Holly corrected.

"No one told me anything. I didn't even see him there!" Ivy turned bewildered eyes on Holly. "What happened? Why didn't Adam tell us about this?"

With hideous clarity, Holly remembered every word of her discussion with Adam. "I think he tried to." She quickly scanned the papers. "It's Mrs. Fitzhugh and the Winter Ball committee. They're suing us over the bills."

Holly wanted to throw herself on her bed and bawl as she remembered the look on Adam's face. He'd quit his partnership for her and she'd criticized him for having principles. "Does anyone know you have these?" she asked Ivy as tears blurred the words on the documents.

Ivy shook her head. "I waited until lunch and took them. There's a whole stack of court papers and I put ours on the bottom. I can pretend I never saw them. Maybe by the time they remember, you can talk to Adam. He wouldn't let them sue us."

"I'm not so sure." Holly stared at the papers and her hands began to shake. "Fraudulent business dealings? That's absurd." She threw the papers on the table.

Laurel picked them up. "We could destroy these."

Holly got wearily to her feet. "I'll take them back. Don't worry, Ivy."

Ivy looked ready to cry. "You'd better let me. I can sneak the papers back and no one will know they've been gone."

"No." Holly smiled sadly. "I've got some groveling to do."

Adam's office was cluttered with signs of packing. Holly tapped on the open door before walking the miles to his desk.

His face was expressionless as he watched her approach.

It seemed best to dispense with the social amenities. Holly carefully unfolded the slightly rumpled papers and smoothed them on his desk, brushing aside a take-out food container. The crackling was the only sound in the room.

"Where did you get these?"

Holly stood, like an errant schoolgirl in front of the principal's desk. "It's quite a coincidence, actually. Ivy's working here as a temp. She was given the papers to type, panicked and brought them to me."

Adam flicked a glance at her before picking up the documents Holly would have given anything to burn. He put them in his out basket, then returned to his writing.

Holly wasn't about to let him ignore her. "This is the case you were talking about yesterday, isn't it?"

Adam dropped his pen and steepled his hands. "Yes."

He obviously wasn't in a charitable mood. "Did you unresign?"

"No."

Holly made a vague gesture that silently asked what he was still doing there. "Just tying up loose ends," he answered.

"I knew Laurel's chummy poses wouldn't sit well with those women, but fraudulent business dealings?"

"Going to play it that way, are you?" Adam leaned back in his chair and reached behind him. He tossed the calendar at her. "Seen that before?"

Bianca, the penthouse, Darlene and...the fireplace tools, logo clearly visible. Holly closed her eyes and exhaled shakily.

"Did you know about that?" Adam asked, his voice rising.

"No!" Holly protested. "Well, afterward," she amended.

"Check February."

Holly saw the notorious red scrap of lingerie and dropped the calendar as if she'd been scalded. Her face flamed. "I didn't know what Gus had planned. You told him he could use the penthouse that day," Holly reminded Adam.

"Good point."

"I didn't tell you about it before because I was ashamed at the way Gus set us up. I walked in on the photo session and threw them out."

"During what month?"

Maybe he didn't hate her completely. "November. Gus must have done December first."

Adam didn't smile, but his face seemed softer. "The calendar gave Mrs. Fitzhugh ammunition to convince her brother to take the committee's case."

Holly bowed her head. "I'm sorry."

"So am I." Adam studied her. "Steele thinks you planned this whole thing as revenge."

Holly shook her head. "Please get them to drop the suit and...and...talk or compromise or whatever you do."

Adam raised one black brow.

"It'll ruin us," Holly pleaded.

"Probably."

Holly waited for a hint of compassion. If she had ever meant anything to him... "Help me."

The bland mask cracked just a little. "I did when I resigned, because I'm very good and I would win."

Holly gasped slightly. "And now?"

"You need a good trial lawyer." Adam cleared his throat. "I'm available, as it happens." His lips curved slightly.

Holly stood a little straighter. Now she understood. It was his career or hers. And Adam didn't hesitate to sacrifice his.

But Holly did. Hours of mind-numbing work, petty humiliations, nagging, cajoling and pushing couldn't be dismissed in an instant. It took two. "Hiring a lawyer would be a pointless waste of money I don't have," she said, deliberately misunderstanding his offer. "I'll just make a simple statement to the judge. That should clear everything up."

"You'll be committing financial suicide." The coolness in Adam's voice was replaced by concern.

"No." Holly gave him a bitter smile as she turned to leave. "I did that last week."

CHAPTER ELEVEN

THEY WERE DESTROYING the woman he loved.

Adam sat toward the back of the courtroom, directly behind Holly, so she'd be unable to see him out of the corner of her eye. He stared at the solitary figure in the conservative navy suit and the unrestrained brown curls. Too stubborn and too proud to accept his offer of help. And he loved her, anyway.

The trial had been scheduled quickly, with Mr. Steele calling in his markers. Adam thought disgustedly of the hundreds of plaintiffs who waited years for their cases to come to trial. Mr. Steele's justification was that the ballet couldn't function without their money from the ball.

He knew that Holly hoped a quick resolution would allow the publicity to die down so she could start over.

Adam shifted on the hard wooden bench as he examined the battery of lawyers clustered around Mr. Steele. So, who was the crown prince chosen to lead the attack against Holly and her small-time business? Joe Longoria.

Adam brightened. Joe was thorough and methodical, but too slow to recognize when a particular strategy wasn't working.

However, this time, his strategy appeared to be working.

Adam mentally winced each time a witness appeared. With no defense lawyer to object, Joe gained confidence as he flirted with the gray areas of courtroom procedure. Adam gritted his teeth until his jaw ached. Anyone who had ever

watched television trials would have been tempted to
scream. "Objection—leading the witness," or, "Objection—irrelevant."

Right now, Mrs. Herman Bloom was testifying.

Joe was posturing. "Describe your dealings with the Hall
sisters."

Mrs. Bloom, an ample woman with small eyes, preened
self-importantly. "Those girls were always looking down
their noses at people."

Objection, sighed Adam mentally.

Joe, in one of his ponderously choreographed moves,
looked to where the jury would be—if there had been a jury.
"You had a business relationship?" he prompted.

Mrs. Bloom sniffed. "Those girls were just playing at
business, you know?"

Objection.

Joe leaned against the witness stand. "No, you tell us."

"They bounced checks all over town. It didn't matter to
them that I had to eat and they had their trust funds. They
figured I could wait for my money." Mrs. Bloom looked
righteously indignant.

Joe strolled over to the exhibit table. "Bank records."

Those were duly entered as Adam got out a small notebook.

"They offered to let me wear their mother's vulgar diamond necklace, like I was a peasant or something."

Adam's heart twisted for Holly. The necklace, even in its
present almost valueless state, was more than a piece of
jewelry to her.

Witness after witness, some who'd had dealings with
Holly and some who hadn't, was called. It seemed at times
that not only Holly, but her family and entire way of life was
on trial. Surely she could see that she was wrong not to have
a lawyer?

After lunch, the courtroom was packed with reporters. News of the juicy trial had leaked out. Holly appeared calm, but Adam noticed her back wasn't quite as straight and her head drooped until she remembered to jerk it upright. Only her hair remained a defiant curly halo around her head.

At least Laurel had taken Adam's advice and stayed home. It would be bad when Joe got around to her sleigh poses, and judging by the expression on Claudia Fitzhugh's face, he was just about to.

"And so out of the generosity of your heart, you gave Holly Hall her big break."

Mrs. Fitzhugh bowed her head modestly. "Her mother was very dear to me." She directed a look of eloquent disapproval at Holly.

"Was Ms. Hall grateful?" Joe assumed his deferential demeanor.

"Apparently not."

"Could you be more specific?"

"She spent thousands of dollars on decorations for the Winter Ball. I'll remind everyone that the primary purpose of the ball is to raise money." Mrs. Fitzhugh addressed the room at large, effectively donning her Old Guard Society Matron guise.

Adam glared at Mrs. Fitzhugh as if he could mentally remind *her* how Holly had come to her rescue twice.

Mrs. Fitzhugh was speaking. "It became like a . . . like a commercial for her sister. And then—" Mrs. Fitzhugh shot a withering look at Holly "—she had the effrontery to bill us for her expenses in promoting her sister's sleazy career."

"Objection!" Adam breathed a sigh of relief at the release he felt. He refused to allow this character assassination to continue.

The crowd of reporters murmured and the judge banged his gavel in the tradition of television dramas.

Adam missed all the looks directed at him, except one. After Holly's head swiveled in his direction in stunned surprise, a huge smile lit her face. Adam's eyes locked with hers as he made his way to the front of the courtroom, oblivious to the judge's beckoning.

Adam wanted to hold her and tell her everything would be all right, but contented himself with grasping both her hands in his. They were cold.

"What are you doing?" The words formed a question, but Holly's voice was a caress.

Adam's eyes searched her face, his lips tilted in a half smile. "I'm your knight in shining armor."

Holly shook her head. "Don't. Mr. Steele will never take you back."

Adam's lips parted with dawning comprehension. "That's why you wouldn't let me represent you?"

Holly dipped her head for a moment, then shrugged lightly. "I couldn't ruin your career," she whispered. "I'm in love with you."

Adam's smile was blinding. "So you were going to sacrifice Deck the Halls." The blood pounded through his veins. "Holly." His voice was husky and his arms ached to hold her, but conscious of their surroundings, he only squeezed her hands.

Adam felt a touch at his elbow. "Hey, man." Joe Longoria tugged Adam away to confront the stern-faced judge.

"Permission to approach the bench," Adam asked belatedly. Reaching into his breast pocket, he withdrew a card and his credentials and presented them. "Adam Markland, with Markland Associates."

The judge peered at the card. "Boston." He looked at Adam over the top of his glasses. "I don't need to tell you that I won't tolerate these shenanigans in my courtroom."

"No, sir." Adam turned icy blue eyes toward Joe Longoria.

"And your client chose not to be represented by counsel."

"My client came here to explain a misunderstanding, not to commit social and financial suicide. She expected matters to be resolved within a few minutes. This lengthy excuse for publicly humiliating her family has changed her mind."

"I'll bet it has," the judge muttered. He banged his gavel and called for a ten-minute recess.

"Adam," Holly began, a few minutes before the recess was over. "I know how you feel about being in the courtroom. It makes you…uncomfortable." She shook her head. "It's okay. You don't have to do this. I wouldn't love you any less."

Adam was surprised into a laugh. "Good!"

"Maybe we could—"

Adam laid a hand over both of hers. "Holly, dear heart, I choose not to be a trial attorney. I think there are better ways. But I've been one. Yes," he affirmed as her face registered amazement. "In fact," he continued in a light conversational voice, obviously enjoying himself, "I'm really quite good. No, I'm the best."

He looked at her with such blazing intensity, in spite of his teasing tone, that Holly believed him instantly.

"It got so other attorneys didn't want to appear against me. They'd knew they'd lose and wanted to settle out of court. I began to prefer that, which irritated my family. They tried to pressure me, so I left. Steele offered me a partnership and I accepted, even though I knew he thought he could talk me back into the courtroom. Look." Adam pointed, his grin almost menacing. "You can see Joe Longoria sweating from here."

"Adam?" Holly said uncertainly.

His face softened instantly. "It'll be okay. Don't worry."

Of course she was going to worry, Holly thought as she listened to more of Mrs. Fitzhugh's attacks. She stole a glance at Adam.

He wore his lawyer face and leaned forward attentively. Mrs. Fitzhugh, lulled by his deferential mask, continued to list her complaints against Holly.

At last it was Adam's turn. "Mrs. Fitzhugh, you sound very different now than you did before and during the Winter Ball. Then you were extremely grateful."

"That was before I discovered how I was used."

Adam straightened and fixed her with an unblinking stare. To Holly's astonishment, a faint pink tinged Mrs. Fitzhugh's cheeks. "How long does it take to plan the Winter Ball?"

"A year."

"Who was contracted to decorate for this year's event—before Ms. Hall?"

"John Kelly."

"Prestigious name—known for his lavish and unusual interiors. Yet he backed out three weeks before the ball, leaving you in danger of canceling, isn't that so?"

Mrs. Fitzhugh nodded reluctantly.

"Please answer audibly. The court reporter can't record gestures."

"Yes." Mrs. Fitzhugh answered through gritted teeth.

"Thank you. Mrs. Fitzhugh, to save time, I will summarize the events that followed. You may speak out if any differ from your recollection."

Holly listened as Adam calmly retold the story of her involvement with the Winter Ball, transforming her from an unscrupulous opportunist furthering Laurel's immoral career into a hardworking businesswoman, too generous for her own good. At Adam's prodding Mrs. Fitzhugh, whose eyes kept darting toward Joe Longoria, periodically confirmed his statements.

"Who pays for the Winter Ball?" Adam leaned back against the exhibit table.

"We sell tickets and there are several underwriters. Businesses donate food, flowers, that sort of thing." Mrs. Fitzhugh eyed him warily.

"And, in fact, Holly Hall donated her services, true?"

Mrs. Fitzhugh nodded.

"Let the record show an answer in the affirmative. Please tell the court what happened when Ms. Hall presented her list of expenses to you." Adam folded his arms across his chest.

Mrs. Fitzhugh's mouth opened and closed. "They were terribly high—higher than I'd expected. I'm sure that in other years John Kelly Interiors must have absorbed some of the costs—"

Adam cut her off. "John Kelly Interiors is an established firm that has an inventory of its own. They may or may not have done as you suggested. Did you pay Ms. Hall's invoice?"

"I . . ."

"Answer yes or no."

"No."

Even though Holly knew the answer, she, along with the rest of the courtroom, followed the exchange in rapt silence.

"Not only did you not pay Ms. Hall, you let her understand that if she pressed you, she would not work in Dallas again."

"Objection," Joe announced.

"I did not!" Mrs. Fitzhugh's chin began to tremble.

Adam ignored him. "Your exact words were: 'Do that and you won't work in Dallas again.' Correct?"

"I don't remember!"

"You are under oath."

"I can't . . ." Mrs. Fitzhugh sent a beseeching look to her brother.

"Words to that effect?"

"I—yes!" She covered her face with her hands.

Adam wasn't finished. "What other firm could put together a first-rate and—by your own admission—the most successful ball ever in three weeks?"

Mrs. Fitzhugh didn't answer. The judge motioned for her to, but Adam broke in. "She can't answer because no other firm could have done it. Holly Hall did the impossible for charity, knowing she wouldn't receive a penny for her labor and then got stuck with the bills because a greedy chairwoman knew she could get away with it."

Adam strode toward Holly as Joe screamed in objection. Mrs. Fitzhugh and Holly wore identical stunned expressions.

Holly laid a hand on Adam's arm. "Did you have to do that?"

Adam, the lawyer, answered her. "Shall I have the court reporter read back all the things she said about you?"

Holly shook her head.

"Hang in there, we're nearly done." Adam went to the exhibit table and got a copy of Holly's invoice, holding it high over his head. "I want it entered into the record that my client made repeated attempts to resolve this conflict and was rebuffed. She generously offered to absorb costs she hadn't expected to, putting herself in financial jeopardy. This trial is no more than blackmail."

Adam strode back to sit with Holly as the courtroom erupted. The judge could no longer tolerate the noise from the reporters and declared a recess. When the trial resumed, half the press was gone.

Holly ran her fingers through her hair as she nervously watched the lawyers huddling around Joe Longoria.

"We've got 'em." Adam regarded the men contemptuously. "The public is on your side now and these guys are exposed for the big bullies they are."

"What's going to happen?" Holly asked.

Adam shrugged. "If they're smart, they'll get out of this quick."

Joe approached the judge. "Your honor, in light of recent developments and the explanation given by Ms. Hall's attorney, we withdraw our suit."

"Bernie," the judge muttered, glaring at Mr. Steele and shaking his head in exasperation, "I can't believe you called me back from vacation and pulled a stunt like this." He banged his gavel as the remaining reporters shuffled out the doors or ran to Holly. The shouted questions blurred together; the camera lights momentarily blinded her. She clutched Adam's arm until a microphone was thrust too close to her face and she released his arm to bat it away. The crowd separated them immediately.

Seeing that Holly was overwhelmed, Adam moved away, drawing half a dozen reporters with him.

In a few moments it was over. Holly dealt ably with the two remaining television crews as Mr. Steele approached Adam. "Reconsider that resignation, Adam?"

"Nope. I'll be vacating the penthouse today."

Mr. Steele shook his head as they walked toward the back of the now empty courtroom. "I knew having you with the firm was too good to last."

"MRS. FITZHUGH DROPPED the suit." Holly wearily set her purse on the kitchen counter and kicked off her pumps.

"I know." Laurel nodded her head. "It's been on the news."

"I expected more of a reaction from you." Holly looked at her sister in surprise.

"I have to talk to you about something. Bart King—with the film commission?—said my pictures have generated a lot of interest."

Holly opened the refrigerator door. "Mr. King has a flair for understatement." Seeing nothing cold to drink, Holly filled a glass with water and ice, collapsed into a chair at the table and waited for Laurel to continue.

"Holly, some casting directors have asked to see me." She tilted her head defiantly and swallowed. "I'm leaving for Los Angeles."

Nothing surprised Holly anymore. Laurel would have to find out for herself what kind of parts she'd be offered, if any. Holly opened her mouth to wish her well, but Laurel, apparently thinking she was going to get a lecture, cut her off.

"I don't want to hear any more about Deck the Halls! I'm sick to death of Deck the Halls! What about *my* life? Ever since Mama and Daddy died, I've done what *you* thought was best. I'm two years older than you were when you had to start running this family." Laurel stopped and took a deep breath. "I'm not going to spend any more of my life pandering to your ego by helping you build *your* business. You want to throw away your money on society snobs, go ahead. I'm not working like a slave to help you do it."

A month ago, Holly would have interrupted Laurel to argue, but the trial had taken all the fight out of her. She wasn't angry; she regretted that Laurel had held these feelings in for so long. "I'll miss you."

A look of disbelief, followed by elation, flickered across Laurel's face before it was smothered by concern. "The news reports were right, weren't they, Holly? It's over? We came out of it okay?"

"If you mean do we have to pay them any of our non-existent money, no. Whether we ever work again remains to be seen."

"I need to pack. Holly?"

"Take what you want, but be reasonable about it."

Holly sipped her water, wishing she had something stronger. Starting Deck the Halls again with just Ivy wasn't going to be the same. Laurel had contributed more than Holly had given her credit for, and she made a mental note to tell her so before Laurel left. And to send her off with the biggest hug she'd ever had...

"I'm glad I caught the news on TV. Didn't you think I'd want to know we're off the hook?" Ivy leaned in the doorway.

"Ivy!" Holly lowered her stockinged feet from the kitchen chair and grimaced. "I'm sorry. So much happened, I forgot that you didn't know."

Ivy crossed her arms, but didn't come into the kitchen. "It wouldn't be the first time you forgot to tell me something important. Or is it that you think I'm too young to know these grown-up things?"

Holly very carefully lowered her glass to the table. "You're right. I should have told you immediately, but I saw Laurel as soon as I stepped in the door and she chose that moment to tell me about all the horrible things I've done that might not have come out in the courtroom where I've spent the entire day." Holly bit out the last words as she ran out of breath. She was close to tears.

"Adam turned out to be an old-fashioned hero, according to the news reports," Ivy said mildly.

Holly sank back in her chair. "He was incredible." It was disconcerting to discover she'd fallen in love with someone she didn't even know.

Ivy walked toward the table. "This came by courier a little while ago."

Holly reached for the envelope, but Ivy snatched it away. "Not yet. I opened it and it's a check from the Winter Ball committee signed by Claudia Fitzhugh. I don't know exactly how much of our expenses it covers, since you didn't bother to tell me how much they were."

"If you'll give it to me, I'll let you know." Holly held out her hand, but Ivy shook her head.

"I want one-third of this."

"Are you willing to take on one-third of our debt, too?" Holly regretted the words as soon as they were out.

Ivy hesitated, then handed Holly the envelope. Quickly doing some rough figuring, Holly said, "This will pay off everything but the silk, which we'll keep, and after paying for that, we ought to have four thousand left over. Total cash assets. You want a third of that now, or plow it back into the business and get all your college money later?"

"Now. I've been talking with some of my friends who are at the University of Texas and they have room for a fourth roommate in their apartment. I'm going to Austin now to get a job and then I'll enroll for summer school."

"You want to go to UT?" Holly tried to hide her dismay. "I assumed—" She caught herself. "They have an excellent business school."

"And journalism department, which is good since I plan to be a sportswriter," Ivy announced calmly.

"You've got it all planned." Holly knew she had to reach deep within herself and show Ivy some enthusiasm. "I'll miss you," she said with sincerity. "And I wish you success. But I'm going to get lonely with both you and Laurel gone."

"You won't be lonely," Ivy said, nodding toward the door behind Holly. "Laurel and I invited company."

Holly turned and saw Adam. He opened the door and shoved two suitcases inside. "Any damsels in distress here?"

"I think the other two can take care of themselves," Holly said, wondering about the luggage.

"Hi, Adam." Ivy gave him a hug, whispered in his ear and discreetly left the kitchen.

"What do you mean you didn't tell her?" Adam called after Ivy, as she scampered up the stairs.

"Tell me what?"

"I was on my way to a hotel, but Laurel and Ivy invited me to stay here." Adam went to the refrigerator, shook his head and got a glass of water. He sat at the table with her. "When they said 'we,' I assumed it included you."

"I'm sorry." She should have remembered that he was leaving the penthouse.

"I'm not." His blue eyes scorched her face.

Holly's numbed senses began to stir, warmed by his look. "There's certainly plenty of room. Laurel is off to California and Ivy is leaving for Austin."

Adam grinned. "Good for them."

"Are you on your way back to Boston?" Holly brought her glass to her lips, trying to fool Adam into thinking it was a casual question.

Adam waited until she set the glass down again, smiling a smile that told her he wasn't fooled at all. "Everything I want is here."

Holly clenched her glass, suddenly nervous. "What about—" she hesitated "—your work?"

Adam watched her with growing amusement. "I'm starting my own firm as I should have done in the first place. Got any space for rent?"

"Here?" Holly's lips curved in a slow smile. "I like that idea. Maybe rent some of the bedrooms to others who—"

"No!" Adam stated firmly. "I'll rent whatever you don't use as storage."

Holly sobered. "I don't know if I'll continue Deck the Halls." She swirled the ice in her glass. "I built it for Laurel and Ivy, you know."

"And for you."

Holly frowned. "They think I'm some kind of slave driver."

"Well, you are."

Holly turned hurt eyes toward him. "I had to be."

Adam smiled gently. "Had. You kept your family together until they could take care of themselves." He stood and offered her a hand, leading her to the family room off the kitchen.

Ivy had left the television on, and Adam turned it off before they were bombarded with more news flashes. He settled Holly on the sofa and drew her next to him. "The fight's over, Holly. You won. It's time they were on their own."

"I know." Holly leaned her head on Adam's shoulder. She pulled the check from her pocket. "From Mrs. Fitzhugh."

"It's a little short."

Holly shook her head. "The difference is about what the silk is worth. That woman doesn't miss much."

"You see? You've got all that silk. You'll have to keep Deck the Halls going," Adam teased gently.

In her mind, Holly replayed bits of the courtroom scene, contrasting that Adam with the familiar one who sat with his arm draped around her. "I don't know you at all, do I?" she finally burst out in a voice filled with self-derision.

Adam tilted her chin with his fingers. "Holly, look at me." Holly did and caught her breath at the expression on his face. "Yes, you do. I'm hardly Adam-the-Barracuda at all anymore. I don't like him very much. You know the real me. No one else ever did."

"I'm sorry you had to do that today—"

"No." Adam shook his head. "It's the best thing that could have happened. Not only did I get you off the hook, I've, uh, proven myself on the Texas battlefield. I shouldn't have to do it again. That day you told me I should take the case—you were right, but for the wrong reasons."

"A nice change from being wrong for the right reasons."

"Like trying to sacrifice everything you'd worked for to save my partnership at Swinehart, Cathardy and Steele." His eyes filled with tenderness.

"Lot of good it did," Holly mumbled.

Adam tilted her chin again. "Yes, it did," he said before his lips descended to meet hers.

The sweetness of his kiss flowed through her, washing away all the hurt and bitterness. "But loving you is right for all the right reasons," Holly whispered against his mouth.

"Definitely." Adam drew her closer. "I love you, Holly," he said, in a voice raw with emotion. "And I've wanted you for so long, but after what you've been through today—"

"Adam," she said, her voice huskier than usual, "*please* take advantage of me."

He laughed and kissed her forehead. "All right—will you marry me?"

"Yes," Holly replied immediately.

Adam's look of pleased surprise was followed by one of such blazing joy that Holly felt her throat tighten. He pulled her to him. "And maybe we could fill some of these bedrooms with little Marklands?'' Adam searched her face as he asked.

Holly grinned. "During the off-season, of course."

"Of course," Adam agreed as he kissed her again, stopping abruptly with a stricken look on his face. "What's nine months from now?"

Holly began to laugh. "Christmas!"

HARLEQUIN

Romance

Coming Next Month

#3097 SOCIETY PAGE Ruth Jean Dale
The last person Annie Page wants to work for is newspaper publisher Nick Kimball, her late husband's sworn enemy. Still, any job is better than none when you're broke. What she doesn't foresee is enjoying the job—or falling in love with Nick.

#3098 LOVE THY NEIGHBOUR Victoria Gordon
Their first meeting was explosive, and Fiona Boyd resolves to avoid millionaire sheep farmer Dare Fraser as much as possible. Realizing her dream of independence proves difficult, however, since Dare turns out to be the man next door.

#3099 A SECOND LOVING Claudia Jameson
Happily engaged to Alan, Emma never questions the strength of her feelings for him until she arrives in America to nurse her convalescent brother. When she meets her brother's blond Viking of a neighbor, Tor Pedersen, there is no need for words....

#3100 BURNING DREAMS Peggy Nicholson
When Kara Tate's father manages to burn down a Stonehall stud barn, Texas pride leaves Jordan Stonehall satisfied that his father's old enemy will rot in jail. But Kara has a plan for restitution—one a man like Jordan Stonehall is honor bound to accept....

#3101 A WOMAN'S PLACE Nicola West
TV producer Marc Tyrell makes it clear that he expects Jan to swallow her principles and acknowledge that he's the boss. But Jan figures men have had their own way for too long—and she has other ideas!

#3102 BOND OF DESTINY Patricia Wilson
Victoria's teenage dreams of marrying Damien Hunt shattered when she discovered that he and her grandfather had planned the marriage for the sake of their family business. She ran away to a new life, but six years later, when Damien finds her again, she can't help but wonder what his motives are this time.

Available in January wherever paperback books are sold, or through Harlequin Reader Service:

In the U.S.
901 Fuhrmann Blvd.
P.O. Box 1397
Buffalo, N.Y. 14240-1397

In Canada
P.O. Box 603
Fort Erie, Ontario
L2A 5X3

Harlequin Superromance®

Hamilton

H·O·U·S·E

A powerful restaurant conglomerate that draws the best and bright-
est to its executive ranks. Now almost eighty years old, Vanessa
Hamilton, the founder of Hamilton House, must choose a successor.
Who will it be?

Matt Logan: He's always been the company man, the quintessential
team player. But tragedy in his daughter's life and a passionate love
affair force him to make some hard choices....

Paula Steele: Thoroughly accomplished, with a sharp mind, perfect
breeding and looks to die for, Paula thrives on challenges and wants
to have it all...but is this right for her?

Grady O'Connor: Working for Hamilton House was his salvation after Vietnam. The war had messed him up but good and had killed his
storybook marriage. He's been given a second chance—only he
doesn't know what the hell he's supposed to do with it....

Harlequin Superromance invites you to enjoy Barbara Kaye's dramatic and emotionally resonant miniseries about mature men and
women making life-changing decisions. Don't miss:

- CHOICE OF A LIFETIME—a July 1990 release.
- CHALLENGE OF A LIFETIME—a December 1990 release.
- CHANCE OF A LIFETIME—an April 1991 release.

Take 4 bestselling love stories FREE

Plus get a FREE surprise gift!

Harlequin Superromance®

THEY'RE A BREED APART

The men and women of the Canadian prairies are slow to give their friendship or their love. On the prairies, such gifts can never be recalled. Friendships between families last for generations. And love, once lit, burns hot and pure and bright for a lifetime.

In honor of this special breed of men and women, Harlequin Superromance® presents:

SAGEBRUSH AND SUNSHINE
(Available in October)

and

MAGIC AND MOONBEAMS
(Available in December)

two books by Margot Dalton, featuring the Lyndons and the Burmans, prairie families joined for generations by friendship, then nearly torn apart by love.

Look for SUNSHINE in October and MOONBEAMS in December, coming to you from Harlequin.

Harlequin romances are now available in stores at these convenient times each month.

Harlequin Presents
Harlequin American Romance
Harlequin Historical
Harlequin Intrigue

These series will be in stores on the 4th of every month.

Harlequin Romance
Harlequin Temptation
Harlequin Superromance
Harlequin Regency Romance

New titles for these series will be in stores on the 16th of every month.

We hope this new schedule is convenient for you. With only two trips each month to your local bookseller, you will always be sure not to miss any of your favorite authors!

Happy reading!

Please note there may be slight variations in on-sale dates in your area due to differences in shipping and handling.

HDATES